THE PINK PAPER FLOWERS

2014-21

RAJ

Made with ❤ on the Notion Press Platform

www.notionpress.com

Contents

'Pain demands to be felt'
PETER VAN HOUTEN
An imperial afflictions

-JOHN GREEN
THE FAULT IN OUR STARS

ACKNOWLEDGEMENTS TO –

THE FAULT IN OUR STARS

SAIRAT –THE MOVIE

KOSALA - THE BOOK

CHAPTER 1

Hometown

(Konkan- Maharastra)

Late June 2014

A same day as usual, to sit on the seashore as every evening and listening waves, with drowning sun. Rain was just stop after two hours and there was moist in air. That was feeling so much comfort. Sea was roaring like the powerful one. Orange, yellow, red colors were spread across the sky.

It was late in June, when everyone was waiting for the results. Diploma exams were ended and result was pending.

Both completed the 3 academic years of diploma in Computer Engineering and looking for further graduation. They both had studied well and hoping for the good grades. To be a successful IT engineer was the dream for both.

Sham and Navin.

Both were the best buddies from childhood. Used to play and study together. They had same school; same diploma collage and now they were also trying to be in same collage. Every day they used to pray for that.

Result declared and both scored good score to get the best collage for further. Everyone was asking 'what's next?

Pune

They were thinking to get the higher education in Pune will be great for the future job. Also Navin's sister who was married, used to live in Pune.

They both filled the form online and give the preferences in Pune collages. The first round list comes out and both got the same collage which was approx. 30 min where the Navin's sister was residing.

They were happy and excited to be in pune. Everything was happening as per they wishing.

After an online completion process they had to visit the collage where the next, documents verification process was about to be.

They packed their stuff and heads towards the Pune.

CHAPTER 2

Pune

They came to Pune. Navin had come two times before in Pune so he was known little about there and Sham who was the new one in the city. He was lot of exited for next period of time.

First, they went to the flat where Navin's sister was residing. Got fresh, had breakfast and then went to the collage. They came in the college campus with Navin's sister's scooter.

"Is it college or university?" Sham asked as he saw the little kids in school uniform and young students too.

"I think so" Navin was also shocked as he saw first time everything was in same campus. There was a huge building in there with different academic departments. Lots of students wear different types of uniforms of different ages. There were also college students wearing casual wears.

"Look they had own ATM machine there." Sham pointed nearby building beside canteen. The private bank's red ATM was inside small room with crowded line.

"They have MBA collage and medical collage too there. Look." Navin points the board which was directing the campus.

After completing admission process they sit in canteen and were discussing about they are at right place for the future. It was reputed collage in Pune having best faculty, huge campus, big library, best computer labs and big canteen too. It was also referred that having a good placements. While admission they got another friend from nearby district Sindhudurga (Konkan) named Jeevan.

Nearby, outside the collage there was a hostel. For the boys which was privately owned. They visited there and confirmed the room for the Sham and Geevan.

Before them, already two students had booked the same room so they two adjust in between them. They were from AhmedNagar. From Mechanical. Kalpesh and Sujit. Navin's sister insists Navin to stay with them.

In evening Sham was telling his mummy and papa how the best collage they got and having so many facilities and the huge campus. He was explaining them about the collage and Pune.

In between Navin came with his sister's scooter and they five went outside to have tea.

Late evening Sham and Geevan unpacks their bags and they went outside for dinner. After a long time Sham was relaxed so much. For him it was like a dream. The best thing was Navin was again with him. The mechanical guys were living in one room and Sham and Geevan were living in Hall. It was small 1 BHK flat. They ended up talking late till 2AM and then sleep.

Whole day they rush in admission process. All were tired. Everyone sleeps. Not one... Sham.

He was missing his home. Mummy, papa, brother, sister and special one. His first love - SEA. It was his best friend from the childhood. Every time he was happy, sad, tired, exhausted, he used to spend it with Navin or Sea. He was missing his roaring sound which used to listen every night from home while sleeping. But he was also feeling good for whatever happening.

"Maybe this will be for a better future". He mumbled and lay on bed to sleep.

There was little breeze coming from window disturb his sleep. Window was not completely closed. Because of rain there was cold outside. He gets up and closed the window.

Pick up the water bottle and come in the balcony. That was cold chilling rainy weather and so much silence that can hear the sound of vehicles running far on highway.

He looked up. The moon was its fullest and glowing. Blinking small red dot was moving in straight line. As it come nearby it get bigger and slowly just passed above from collage and landed nearby airport. He surprised, he did not get that whole day that there were lot of planes just fly above them. He looked in mobile. It was 2.30 AM.

"Will be late in morning" He came again on bed and closed his eyes.

Collage start.

From 8.30 AM To 4.30 PM the long eight hours of student's life start again. Last 3 months Sham used to get up late in morning so it became hard to get up in morning. And walk for 10 min and then whole day sitting on bench became boring.

First week passed having introduction of subjects. Five subjects in between three were practical's.

After the collage all came near the snack center which was near the hostel and order Teas. They sit there for half hours just talking and then went to room. Everyone was telling how their previous days, their background and the things happen in their life and future plans too.

On Sunday Navin made a plan with Sham to roam in Pune. Geevan also joined them.

All three get ready and pick up the bus towards Pune. Navin known some places but still was confused about there. They reach PMC (Pune Municipal Corporation). There was old theatre behind them and then Navin didn't get that at which direction last time he went to the Fort-Shaniwar-wada.

He went to nearby shop but there was something written in white paper poster stops him. 'It will cost to ask the address.' The typical puneri pati (Poster).

There was around 50 years old man standing nearby them having newspaper in his bag and big glasses wearing white shirt and black pant. Navin went to him

"Umm...Where is Shanivar-wada?" Navin asked him.

He looked at Navin as he asked him something confidential information. Sham and Geevan behind them were trying to listening where is going to be direct.

"Five rupees" He said without changing his facial expression. All three started to look at each other.

"NO sir, I am asking, how we can go to the Shanivar-wada" Navin asked him again as he think he gets might listen wrong something.

"Are all of you are new here?" That man asked.

Navin was thinking in his mind 'why the hell he asked him' and Sham and Geevan just 'why the hell he is asking.'

"Listen boys, this is Pune. Here you will get nothing free, not even advice. Look at that pati (Poster)" and he direct the shop where Navin previously went. "We are just like the way we are. But still go upstairs by this and on left side you can have 'your' Shanivar-wada." He points towards the stairs made by the black stone.

"Anything else?" That man added with touching his glasses.

Navin, Sham and Geevan were just figuring out they should pay him or not. Navin was about to put his hand in pocket trying to get money. That man just smile and,

"I was joking about the money. Have a good day. Beware from the pocket pickers and careful about the mobile if you have" And he rush as his bus may be arrives.

"Thank you sir" Navin just said with smiles and looked at the Sham.

"Punekar I think" Sham said. "I have read about them in books."

"Yup" Navin wrapped his arm around Navin shoulder.

The climb the stairs at which that gentleman point out and suddenly Navin shout "There it is, I got that"

There was the bridge; on the other hand there was Shanivar-wada. Navin remembered. They crossed the bridge. Gets the ticket and entered in it.

"This is it?" Sham was surprised as he was imagining there would be something big inside of that huge metal gate.

"This used to be big seven story's high building but get burned and destroyed." Geevan answered. Sham looked at him with the short eyed and how he know.

"I read somewhere in newspaper about it" Geevan understand his face and gave the explanation. Sham looked straight and starts to walk.

"You know, it's haunted". Geevan added.

"What?" Sham asked as he was not listening to him.

"Not now, at the night" Navin looked at him and blink his eye. Geevan gets that.

"What?" Sham asked them again as he didn't understand their conversation.

"Climb the stairs. Rocks. Careful." Navin points Sham to distract from the gossip which they reserved for night.

"I'm not kid but..." Sham looked back at Navin. "Why the hell they made so much height of stairs. It can tear my jeans in between" Sham was climbing the stairs with heavy breathe.

"Come on young man you are not a kid. It's just 20 stair and you ..." Navin was poking him on his butt.

The view was really good one. Mula-Mutha River. Front side statue was the looking glorious. They clicked some photos and then came outside after wandering all fort.

After they came in front of the famous Dagadusheth Ganapati temple and then come on the Laxmi road. There was so crowd they think they shouldn't enter in that.

"Where is ABC Chauk?" Sham asked there someone.

"Go behind lane." He replied in hurry.

They came in the ABC Chauk. There were a lot of book shops and Sham was looking for something. He found it. At the end of lane there was signal and beside that shop named ADARSHA BOOK DEPO.

"I want to buy some second hand books" He asked shop owner who was reading book. Aged sixty plus, wearing white shirt and blue jeans, big numbered glasses and looking like retired teacher.

"Go backside and pickup books which you want." That owner said without looking at Sham. He was involved deeply in that book. Sham looked at him astonishingly.

Sham came to the backside of shop. There was thousands of book but no one there. He come at front again and asked. "I want novels"

Shop owner hardly looked at him and said. "Find yourself son".

Sham came again backside of the shop. But again get confused. He didn't get which side he should start. He gets to the end of the sets. Start to choose in between them. He open one by one, glanced at them, pickup five to six books which looks like the novels.

He come in front side of shop and put the books on the table. Shop owner place the book aside and made face like Sham disturbs him while it was interesting.

"Total Price of the books is 600 RS So 300 RS should be." Shop owner said by moving his fingers on calculator.

"300 RS? ..." Sham looked at the books and pick the big one aside and then asked "How much now?"

Owner looked at him and said "Will be 200 RS." Sham gets 100 RS two notes from the pocket and gives to him.

"And this one..?" He asked him curiously.

"I will get that next time..." Sham responded and waves his smile.

"You sure will be there when you will come next time..?"

"I don't know but..." Sham paused for the ....

"Read it, it's a great book." That man looked at him for a second and pick up the book and place in that set and said with crooked smile.

"I didn't have much money and there are already five, so, OK." Sham said while he placed his hand over the books and pickup that book.

"Pay the next time. I am here every day..."

"NO ...BUT..." Sham again stopped while talking.

"It's ok son, you came for the books and I will feel bad if you didn't take ..." That owner was a really good man.

"Ok...I will pay you next time surely..." Sham promised him with the big smile.

That man takes the 200 RS and places it in drawer and start to read the book. Sham picks up books and looked at him. Sham was about to leave, Turns back.

"Can I ask something..?" Sham touches his face with fingers and asked him.

"Haa..." That man looked at him.

"You don't think the books behind there, someone will steal it?" Sham asked him nervously. "Means at night, they will be still here so..."

That man looked at him. He smiles. It was his generous.

"Those books are there from last 17 years and I don't think there will someone steal anything in it. If there, I will be happy if he read it..." Sham smile as he finds out that man has wisdom. He also smiles.

Navin and Geevan at the end of lane were looking for Sham. They all were hungry now. They come nearby hotel and order missal pav for three.

After that Navin planned to spend the time in mall. Pick up the returning bus and the in middle, they stopped. The come into the mall.

It was the first time Sham was entering in the mall. As he never came out of the district, it was all new for him. Beautifully design front entrance, Security check, escalators, English music, classy design, foreign brand shops and foreigners. The smell was there different kind of. The air has something specific aroma in it. It was cold but feels like he is in the factory of chocolates.

He fills like he has come somewhere else. He was looking with wide eyes everything like paradise to him. It was all beautiful.

"Don't look like that, be normal." As Navin saw Sham was looking everything like small child and grabbed his hand.

"It is really looks like I am in America." Sham said looking at Navin with an exciting face. The half skirt white skin skinny lady and his may be his boyfriend passed beside them. Sham was looking at them with the open mouth.

Geevan was looking at Sham and gets that he never came to place like this.

"Hold my hand" Navin groped Sham's hand and start to walk. Geevan was laughing on them.

"Let's go on there" Sham points towards the escalators.

"We are here for two hours now, don't run like child." Navin shout. As he says Sham who didn't listen him start to pull him.

Next two hour all three of them just walking, walking and walking. This was a greatest experience for him. He was looking at everything with curiosity. They clicked lots of photos in there. First time he saw the price of the suit in the price of whole family cloths.

Somewhere Sham said to have a tea but looked at the menu and put it back. It was 150 RS for tea and 250 RS for coffee. He didn't look below that. They come out of the mall.

There was a snack center near the road signal. They get the special tea for 10 RS and cookies. Pick up bus again and return to the room. All day they just walk. Tired. Lay off their body on bed and sleeps as they were feeling pain in their feet.

He was running in mall. There was no one in there. Empty. He shouts "Navin. Look at this". And he just runs. He just stumble something, as he didn't see it...

Sham gets up as he get that he had a dream.

Perfumes smell, popcorn smell, coffee smell. He smiles as he had his best day.

Third semester

First week was about to end. Collage start regular.

"Again you late, this is third time in this week. Navin said furiously when lecture's ends and they were going to have breakfast in canteen. They ordered poha and tea and sits on canteen chair.

"Relax, It will not happen again," Sham said while having sip of tea. Recess was around 15 min. They completed their breakfast and start to walk towards the classrooms.

Sham put a pack of biscuits in front of the puppies who were at the back side of canteen. There was 5-6 Puppies.

Black, brown, white. Chubby and cute.

Lecture start. About five minutes,

Reflection coming on his eyes disturbs him. Because the bike, park outside of building. Sunlight was passing through the mirror into the window, towards the classroom.

But Sham notices something. That reflection was passing through the long shiny hair looking brown because of the sunlight. He notices her. First time. She was sitting on next row to him in forward near window.

Sham lost looking at her.

He lost his concentration when he get hit something on head. Professor notice that, Sham was not paying attention and looking somewhere else. He hit with chalk.

"Where are you looking young man, I am here." Professor say as he caught Sham was looking outside which was really looking at her. All class was looking at him.

Sham was stunned. Now he was looking at professor.

Suddenly, he again gets pleasantly surprised as moves his eyes in that direction again. That girl was looking at him and smiling with tiny corner of her mouth.

God...She is so beautiful and her smile.............., Sham just forgot he was sitting in class room and whole class with professor was staring at him.

"Excuse me" Professor said loudly and Sham breaks his eternity. "You can go outside to wander if you feel bored."

"Sorry sir." Sham said endearingly.

"Pay attention" He warns him.

Professor starts his lecture where it was disturbs.

Sham wanted to see in that direction again but don't want to get ashamed again in front of whole class again.

Lecture ends. Professor left. He looked at her. She was talking with her friend. Suddenly she looked back. Sham feels awkward. She smiles. He also smiles. The first smile they both shared.

"Late and now you were looking outside." Navin hit on his head with notebook.

"There was big pigeon out there." Sham finger towards the window.

"You come to see pigeon or study?" Navin asked.

Professor entered in classroom. Everyone stands up.

Lecture start. Everyone was paying attention. Sham notices something again. She was biting his nails. In her arm there was single gold bangle. Suddenly some hairs swept over her eyes she moves by her hand backside of ears. There was a silver earrings in her ear was adding beauty in her face.

Flawless........She was beautiful.......

Navin hit him with his corner of hand and reminds him he is in lecture. Sham gets that, and starts to look at board.

While lunch break Navin ask him what was outside so much that he was looking. Sham said nothing and smiles.

Third session starts.

Sham, Navin and Geevan entered in classroom. Sit on his desk. He looked at right. She was not there. Someone else was. He looked at front. And then back. She was not there.

She entered in classroom with her friend. As there previous seat was got by someone else, they both went backside of classroom.

Professor enters in class. Lecture start. Whole lecture Sham pays full attention. Lecture ends. Sham looked back. She was talking with her friend.

"She looks like Tabu." Sham talks with himself.

"What...? " As Navin didn't get what was Sham said.

"Nothing..." Sham moves front.

Day ends.

Everyone came out of the campus. They all gather at the snack center where they used to drink tea. They all were talking about the day, fun and jokes.

"Whole day you warc not paying attention on lecture, First getting late and now..." Navin was angry on him.

"Last night I was reading book, sleep late so whole day was dizzy." Sham explains.

"Then sleep early." Navin gives the solution.

"Will do tonight" Sham said while taking a sip of tea.

"Excuse me?" Someone asked who was not from their group.

There was a guy wearing white t-shirt, blue jeans and 2-3 bags in hand. Simple rectangular black frame was on his eyes. Looking like decent guy. He was asking to Geevan

"Yes." Geevan said.

"Where can I find a room or hostel something here. I am from Mechanical and late admission." He share his problem.

"Boys hostel is behind this complex. Ask there." Geevan show the finger and tells him where to go.

In between the others boys from Mechanical asked. "Which division.?"

"C"

"Let's go, I will show you." Sujit and Kalpesh get up. And pay their bill and they three start to walk towards the hostel.

"It's really late to get hostel room. Already full. Last day someone came but didn't get any vacancy. But still try..." Kalpesh said him.

After some time all three came back.

"What happened?" Navin asked them.

"Hostel is full, there is no vacancy there." That new guy said.

"Can we adjust him?" Sujit asked with little generosity.

"But kaka will not agree on it." Geevan said.

"We asked them they say OK but his rent will be added in it. He is in mechanical. It will be good if he stay with us."

"I am from Nagpur and I came directly with the bags so I don't want to stay outside tonight. Kaka said if there will someone left from the hostel they will adjust there." That new guy continued. Sham looked at Geevan. Geevan just nod.

"Ok. It seems to be you really need room. So we will not disappoint you." Sham said.

"Thank brother." He said

"Ohhh by the way, Abhijeet." He introduces himself and handshakes Sham.

"Sham"

"Geevan"

"Navin, but I don't stay with them. Sham is my friend."

"Two teas please...." Sham said towards the shop counter. One for Abhijeet and extra one he wanted. All they went to room. Mechanical boys share their room with Abhijeeet.

*7 August

I saw a girl. Wearing black skater dress. Really looking good. She was there beside my bench. She is pretty. She has beautiful earrings.

@At night around 11 PM.

Sham was reading. As the books continued to female character description, that girl sitting on bench near him, her hair, that reflection came in front of his eyes. He still remember how she was smiling when professor were scolding him. He smiles on himself.

He gets up and comes in the kitchen. Abhijeet comes out of the room wearing black hoodie and grey shorts pant. His hand was in pockets.

"Hey, not sleep yet?" He asked.

"Nopc" Sham answered while drinking water.

"Ok, Will be there in few minutes, don't lock the door"

"Ok." Sham said "But where are you going?"

"For the walk" Abhijeet answered.

And he just walked away from room.

Sham surprised that he didn't even ask to join him. But he think maybe he will have personal reasons like talking on phone or something else maybe. Sham lay on bed.

In half hour, Abhijeet came and lock the door.

"Not yet..?" He asked as Sham was still reading book.

Sham just smiles.

He goes straight in kitchen. Wash his hands and face and went to his room. There was little burning smell around him.

Next day

Everyone comes in lecture room.

Sham entered. Take look in the classroom. She was seating in second bench and bench behind her was empty. He grab Navin's hands and pulled him. He sits on the bench behind her. He was sure at least today he will not get hit by chalk on his head.

Lecture starts. Sham was paying attention on lecture in between he looked at her face. He sits in backside opposite direction so he can see her face.

Two lectures ended. Everyone came to canteen. Get the order and sit on the tables. Abhijeet joins them.

"Isn't she beautiful?' Navin asked while drinking tea.

Sham looked at him. He didn't get it.

"Who?" He asked as he thinks Navin was talking about someone.

"The girl who was sits in front of me. Last day on right and then back side." Navin tell him in just one line and raised his eyebrows. Sham gets it. He smiles.

Abhijeet who was listening them look over Sham. His face was without an expression. Idle.

"Shut up." Sham completes his formality.

"We are here for the study, Right?" Navin drink his tea.

"I know." Sham said heavily.

"Focus on study, two days you are just looking at her." Navin was teasing him.

"Yes sir." Sham said and joins his hand. Abhijeet was trying to show he was unaware of their conversation and finish his breakfast. They all start to walk.

"He seems to be odd one. Last night he goes outside at night, comes late, alone." Sham said to Navin when Abhijeet left them.

"So? May be his girlfriend's call" Navin presume his possibilities. Sham nods.

"Fast, we have to pick up seat" Sham start to walk fast as he reminds something.

"Go and get the seat." As Navin again tease him.

Navin enter in classroom. Sham was on front bench.

"You take study so seriously?" Navin sit beside him.

"There were no benches left and back side we can't listen." There was sorrow in his voice.

"Good" Navin thumbs up.

Day end

They all had tea and come to the room.

Abhijeet unpack his bag. There was induction stove and some small utensils. He inserts the plug in the socket.

"Maybe this will help for tea or coffee." Abhijeet said while starting the button. It beeps and starts to make the sounds like it's working.

"Maggi..." Someone from behind said.

"This is the best." Geevan said as he was fond of coffee. And hate the tea because of its watery taste at stall.

And now Abhijeet becomes everyone's best friend.

@About an 11

Sham was reading book sleeping on stomach. Door open and someone walk away. Closed the main door and went outside.

Sham gets up. Come into balcony. Abhijeet was walking with his hand in pocket of his hoodie.

Sham looked up. Moon was fullest. There were stars blinking. There was a plane in front of him was about to land on airport. There was cold in because of rain. About 30 min later Abhijeet comes. Locked door and went to kitchen. Sham follows him.

"Not sleep yet?" Abhijeet asked while washing his hands.

"You smoked?" Sham attacks on him.

"Yeah" Abhijeet answer while washing his face. Little late reply.

Abhijeet went to his room. Sham drinks a glass of water and sit on the bed. He was little doubt about Abhijeet like he was little mysterious type guy.

Next day Sham told to Navin about it. Navin was surprised because he used to think Abhijeet is a nice guy because he also wears the glasses.

"Drinks...?" Navin ask as he worried about him.

"I don't think so but who knows." Sham said.

"You keep distance from him, If you go with him I will beat you later, first tell to mummy, papa." Navin said while grabbed his neck. Sham was laughing.

"I am serious." Navin was looking angrily.

Actually Navin was worried about the Sham, because Sham was not with him all time. And Sham was little bit obsessed with cigarette. He used to think it is cool. His favorite actor looked so much macho while smoking.

@At night around 11

Abhijeet came out of his room. Sham was waiting for him. He was little curious about Abhijeet. As Abhijeet start to walk out of room, Sham calls him

"Abhi..."

Abhi stop and start to look at him.

"Can I give company?" Sham asked.

Abhi did not say anything. Sham Put bookmark and close the book. Put it on table and starts to walk with him. There was a rain outside. They get their umbrellas and come outside. There was chilling cold outside.

They start to walk. No one was talking. After 10 min they come near highway, crossed road. There was hotel; in front of it was a paan shop. They went there. Abhi tell something to shop keeper. He gives him cigarette. He lights it and start to drag it.

"You want anything paan or chocolate, candy something?" As he gets Sham is with him, he stops smoking and asked him.

"No I am ok" Sham said.

Abhi start to smoke again. He was looking like the movie guy. Bright face, glasses, hoodie, and a serious face which was unable to read what's inside he is thinking.

He completes his cigarette. They start to walk again.

"Everything is ok?" After 2 min Sham breaks the silence. Abhi looked at him and smile and nod his head.

"Why you smoke?" Sham asked him as he was little curious about him. Abhi again didn't say anything.

"It's injurious. People die because of smoking" Sham continues.

"People also die with other reasons too." Abhi explained as he tells him like a philosophy in deep voice.

"But people do not throw themselves to die with the reasons." Sham counter questions.

Abhi stay quiet. They both came to room.

Next day Sham told Navin about this. Navin gets angry and pulled his hand and grabbed with nails in his hand, scratch him. There were three red scratches. Navin was really angry.

"Listen" Sham shout and was trying to save himself.

"I don't want to listen anything. Just don't go with him. Else don't talk with me." Navin start to walk furiously.

"He is nice guy just there will be something. And I don't have any reasons to smoke." Sham was telling him while laughing. Navin was still walking fast. He stops. Look back.

"Everything just starts for fun and then it became habit. And it takes lots to avoid it. Why am I am talking, I am going to tell your papa." Navin gets angry again and leaves him. Start to walk rapidly.

They both come in classroom. She was there. Luckily behind her bench was empty. They both sit there. She was talking with her friend. Suddenly she looked back. Sham who was looking her gets stumped.

She looked at him and gives smile. Sham was just like lost like quantum realms. Navin kicked him and het get back. He revert smile.

Professor entered in the classroom. She turned forward and all students stand ups. Next whole two lecture his eyes were on her.

Day ends.

They all came at the snack center. As regular, they order teas. Geevan and Abhijeet didn't order the tea. Instead they get the milk packet assuming that it will be cost same as tea. They all were talking. Navin interrupt.

"Abhi, Sham told you smoke." Abhi looked at the Sham, As Sham looked another direction. Everyone was surprised as they were not aware about it. Geevan was like why the guy who wears specs and looks like intelligent guy, will be smoker.

"You really smoke. That's why it smells when you return at night." Sujit asked. "I hate that smell." Kalpesh added.

"Don't do that on room, we luckily get the room which is really closed to collage and don't want to throw out." Kalpesh added.

"Yes but it will not happen on room." Abhi told while he was looking at below with nervousness.

"It's OK, Just don't get along with Sham with you." He said while looking at Sham. His eyes were so much rage that for a second Sham scared.

"Ok" Abhi said.

Everyone was silent. Sham breaks it. "There is hotel near highway, let's go out today. This same dal rice, I got bored. There are Chinese dishes too."

"In" Geevan said.

"I am also coming." The Mech guy says.

"Me too" Another one said.

"I will also come." Navin also agreed here.

At night they all went hotel. They were talking while eating. Abhi finished his meal, gives money to Sham and came outside. Smoked cigarette. Everyone finishes their meal. Pay the bill. Come outside. Abhi was waiting for them. They all start to walk with two groups.

"Talk with her." Navin said. Sham and Abhi looked at him as they three were walking group. They both didn't get it.

"I am talking about the girl, you idiot." Navin slap lightly on Sham head. Abhi get relaxed.

"Why?" Sham was just making hype.

"She likes you. Didn't you see she smile today." Navin said.

"She smiles because I am idiot who got scold for not paying attention in lectures. Don't you remember 3-4 Days back?" Sham reminds him how may be she thinking about him.

"I know but today she was not smile as you look idiot. Talk with her." Navin put his arm around his shoulder and said.

Abhi gets uncomfortable as he let them walk together and stay back. The conversation seems about to end.

"And what about you?" As Navin turn back and asked Abhi.

"What" As Abhi didn't get that 'why' Navin asked him.

"Cigarettes, Any problem?" Abhi waves his head in No and didn't tell anything.

"Sort out it. Cigarettes will not help. And keep this idiot away" Navin said and again stared at Sham.

They reached at their hostel. Navin start his scooter and went. All five they come on room. When Abhi was going in his room, Sham calls him from balcony. Abhi comes in balcony.

They both stand there for long time. Looking at sky. It was clear but still cold in air. Sham wants to ask him but he stay silent. May be Abhi is not that closed to him ask about. After some time they think will be late so came inside.

"You have any problem while sleeping?" Abhi asked him as he everyday just try hard to sleep early but ended up late.

"Yeah. Facebook internet..."

"Listening silent songs may help. Only 2. But will relax your mind. Try." Abhi tell him as may be he used to do it every day.

"Ok" Sham flicked his eyebrows.

Abhi went his room. Sham remembers. He used to listens a song from movie 'Sarfarosh' That silent gazal. He puts on his headphone. Start song. As the song moves forward Sham gets that lyrics are familiar and he end up remember her face again.

*Her beautiful smile.

After three times, He put his headphone aside and closed his eyes. He just don't get when he sleeps.

Next day

While going collage, Sham told Abhi that it was a good hack to get sleep. Abhi asked him does he remember someone or just listens song as always. Sham didn't say anything but as the way he makes his face Abhi gets that.

Lecture start. It was so boring that everyone was trying hard to stay awake. She was sit at backside so Sham can't see her. Whole lecture he was just looking front. Lectures end. Everyone went to canteen.

For the next session they come near the classroom. As always they were late but there was no one in classroom. Someone come outside from nearby HOD cabin and saw them standing out there. He went to them.

They were HOD.

"All students are in computer labs. Practical's started onwards. Don't get late again." With adjusting his tie they said.

Sham, Navin and Geevan runs towards the computer labs. Looking for every board on the doors, they found it. They get welcome by clapping and cheering from other student's for getting late. All three were lower their head as embracement and sit on the backside of the room. She and her friend was sitting backside of the class.

Practical ended early by half an hour as it was introduction and the semester timetables. So they get relaxed. They all were talking with each other and some of them discussing about the syllabus, assignments, chapters and lots more.

She was talking with her friend. Sham and Navin was just sitting behind them. Sham was looking at her. Suddenly she looked back. Sham gets stunned. He was looking in her eyes.

Her deep black eyes.

She looked front but again she looked back and said "You are the one who always been getting late."

As Sham surprised as she was talking with him. He was not in state to talk.

"Yeah, He is lazy one. Sleepy duck." Navin said as Sham was just looking at her and didn't speaking for like a five seconds. Navin kicked his leg on his legs.

"Not every time...." As Sham said and paused as he gets that they were right...

"Maybe" She smiles again.

This is the first time Sham was seeing her face to face and he did not believe that she was talking with him.

She was typical Indian brown face, wearing little nose pin was adding a different kind of beauty in her face. There was small black bindi on her forehead. She was looking amazing.

"Sham." "AnuRadha ..Call me Anu.."

"Navin" "Pooja"

"Geevan"

They all introduce each other. And then their conversation starts from academic to personals.

"Where are you from" Anu asked.

"Sorry?" As Sham was not listing what she said. All he was just looking at her.

"Your hometown?" Anu again asked.

"Guhagar, Ratnagiri, Konkan." Sham tells her full address.

"Konkan , Its really beautiful place to be hometown. Lot of beaches. Once we went there for school trip. It was really awesome. Right Pooja?" Anu looked at Pooja and said.

"Yeah it's really beautiful. And that red Ganesh temple.... White Beach... Amazing view...." Pooja said as she remembers the Ganapatipule temple.

"Maybe we should go again?" Pooja said while looking at Anu.

"Why not." Navin casually invite them.

"How far is beach from your home?" Anu asked as she was thinking they used to live near the sea.

"By walk 5 min" Sham said.

"Isn't it really cool you just go there and sit, looking at the wide sea." Anu said while she places her head on the hand and starts looks in zero.

"Yeah, It's really great but sometime it's really hard to get sleep at night." Sham said.

"We used to go everyday there and play football on beach." Navin told.

Anu and Pooja were best friends from childhood. They share the same colony and their mummy papa were good friends to each other. They complete their education together. And now they enter in this engineering collage again. Pooja was bright in studies so she would help to Anu in studies and that why they were like a sisters. Pooja had scooter so Anu used to fill the petrol. While she was telling she shares the funky smile. She tells everything in between them.

Bell rang and practical ends. Everyone pick up their bags and comes out of the lab. Anu and Pooja were walking in front of them. Sham and Navin were walking keeping distance.

"So, she likes the beaches and konkan. May be she will like someone from konkan." Navin teased Sham.

"Shut up and walk." Sham was showing he was angry but inside he was so much feeling better whatever just happens.

Next session starts

She was sitting on the second bench. Sham was behind them. Her hair ware coming on her face and with finger she was adjusting them behind the ear. As sham was looking at her earing he didn't get that when professor stop his lecture and stand beside him. The whole class was holding his breath. As Sham get that something is wrong he looked up and professor face was filled with such anger that the 'sorry' word just come out of his mouth.

"Go and sit on the first bench which is empty." Professor said and point on front.

As Sham gets its own fault, without talking anything, he gets up and sits on the first bench.

"From onwards you will sit on first bench in my lecture. No one will sit there. This bench will be reserved for him only." Professor was really angry with all week frustration, he punish him single time that Sham going to pay the whole semester. As he caught him third time for not paying attention in lecture.

Sham was looking furiously at Navin. Navin was looking at him with zero expression. The whole lecture Sham only sit on first bench.

Three hours session ends. Day ends.

Navin come and smile. "You..., don't you just kicked when he was stands near me." Sham asked.

"I was." Navin said.

"Now the whole semester I am going to sit on first bench" Sham said nervous tone.

"Did I tell you look at other while lectures?" Navin give his clarification. "At least you are going to be topper onwards."

Everyone was leaving from class room.

"Tea?" As Sham ask to Anu, when she walks near.

"3 Hours was long time to sit in front." Anu said as she knows why Sham gets the punishment and also she doesn't want to upset him. "OK".

They all come in canteen. Sham and Navin gets tea and Anu and Pooja gets the coffee. In mind, they both Sham and Navin were thinking same. From the next, they will drink the coffee only. Finish their beverages and gets up.

"Don't get late tomorrow." While leaving Anu looked at Sham and said and crack the smile. Sham was faking his smile.

"Don't worry he has his reserved bench." Navin said loudly and Sham grabbed up his neck. Pooja start the scooter and Anu sits behind her. They leave. Sham was looking at her.

*11 August

Today we talked. She has a pretty face and great voice.

And we had coffee too. It was a best day I think..

At night Sham went again with Abhi to give him company to walk.

Next day

Sham and Navin comes early and sit on third bench. The front bench was empty. Behind them Anu and Pooja were. The last day professor comes in room. First lecture was on him.

He looked at Sham and with the hand they tell to sit him on first bench. With an upset face Sham gets up and came in front. Navin also get up and was about to sit beside him.

"Not you." Professor said politely.

"I have hearing problem." Navin made up.

As professor gets that he fakes it and 'why he did not sit there in first time' He thinks it will not make any problem to sit there.

"You could have sat there before but fine I don't have any issue with that." He starts his lecture.

Sham and Navin sit on first bench. For Sham it was frustrating but for Navin he thinks it was good.

Next day

Sham gets up. There was no one in room. He looked in his mobile and he was half hour late. He gets ready in 15 minutes and starts to walk towards the collage.

It was practical. He showed up there. Professor asks him why he was late. Sham tells his bike was punctured. Navin, Geevan, Anu, Pooja all were laughing. Professor said OK and tells him to sit. Practical finish.

"You keep your tradition." Anu turned and said while Sham sits behind her.

"Bike... haan...?" Navin asked.

"What if they asked about bike?" Anu asked.

"Navin come with the bike, I would showed his bike." Sham said confidently.

"And, keys?" Navin asked.

"I was sitting backside." Sham told. "Geevan, why don't you get me up?" Sham looked at him and asked.

"We call you three times. You were fast asleep. We think you may have beautiful dream so don't want to disturb you." Geevan give him explanation.

All start to laugh. Sham made face like humiliate in front of girls. They were so loud that professor gives him warning.

"Completed your dream?" Navin asked.

"Attendance" Sham told. "Point" Geevan pat his back and reward him.

*13 August

She is making fun of me for being late, again and again

They all become best friends. The got to know each other very well and exchange their mobiles numbers too. They used to roam in group.

Lectures were happening. Practical's too. Sham only used to be relaxed while practical. In lectures he still forced to first bench. But he gets used to it. In off period they used to sit in library, completing assignments and at the day end, in canteen with coffees.

On room, they five also become very good friends. They told to Abhi not to change the room. He was one of the bright among three of them. He was the problem solver of every equation so it became very helpful to them. Sham was also think that Abhi is his best friend but don't want to tell him nor to Navin. They used to eat together, roam together, watch movie on laptop. And once they all went to Pune have a good time. Where Sham returned the book seller's remaining money and buys another 5 books. Buy the hoodie too. Everything was really going all well.

Three months passed. First prelims completed. There was about 6 days holidays so all they went home. After three months Sham was at home. Everyone in family was happy. They asked a lot about the collage, Pune, Studies, how they lived, everything. Sham was also telling them about all this. Sham was feeling happy for coming home. All he was missing from long time the mom's food. The specially fish curry and rice. And tell not to cook dal till he is there. He was bored for eating dal. After a long time he sleeps so much peacefully in his bed lately. All he was missing for a long time.

At Navin's home they were happy too. His sister also wants to come home but she can't make it. She sent lots of food item that she made and lot of gift to each of them by Navin.

Around 6 PM

He went on the beach after sleeping for long time. 3 months later he was on beach. He feels relaxed. He was listing the song of the sea. He sat on sand. Put his hand in in. Hold it. Only he can know how it was meant for him. He was looking in front. The round red was about to enter in the line.

Navin came. Sit beside him. He did not talk anything. They just sit there and lost in the nostalgia. All they can do is to save all this for next time when whey will come again.

"Feeling really peaceful" Navin said.

"After a long time" Sham gives him smiles.

That round red just lost slowly under the line.

Navin mobile phone rings. He pick up. And start to talk. After some time he give to Sham and said "Talk".

"Who" As he don't know make the call for him.

"Pooja" Navin answered.

Sham was not aware of this. He gets the phone. And start to talk. After talking for some time, he gives it to Navin. Again Navin talk for five minutes. He hung up the call.

Sham looked at Navin.

"What?" Navin asked.

"It's really happening?" Sham asked.

"We used to chat but not on calls. At 4 I call her but she was busy so she returned callback now. Nothing else" Navin explained.

"It great..." Sham said and smiles.

"It's not how you think, we don't used to call. She just tell me when we will reach, text her. I didn't make it so call her few hours ago." Navin was telling him.

"Still, it great...." Sham wishes for him.

After some time, Sham stand up. He removed his sandals and starts to walk in front in sand. He stopped. Cold water was passing in between his legs. He was feeling it.

Holidays ends. All 6 days Sham lived fullest. He used to sleep lately. Eat his favorites. His old friends used to meet them at school in evening. They used to play cricket, football on beach. Sometimes they used to go for small trips on bike and unlimited stories of each other's.

But he was also missing the collage, Mostly Anu. They didn't used to talk on phone. Whenever he feels low, he used to sit on the beach. Listening waves. It was relaxing for him.

They made the reservation for the bus and returned to Pune.

Results were out. Everyone was had a good score. They celebrated it in the canteen with little snacks. All of them were happy. Navin and Pooja now used to sit together. Sham would be uncomfortable while sitting beside the Anu. He still can't talk with Anu as Navin used to talk with Pooja. Anu was a little bit of talkative girl so she was talking clearly on any situation but Sham feel awkward in. He feels like he may talk something wrong and it will embarrass himself.

She was talking with him freely. Lots of time she shares the little things about her. But Sham was never would tell anything that he really feels, He don't want to lose her.

Two times a week he would get scold for getting late in lecture from her. Professor now gets used to it as he will never change. In between Sham get distracted from study. Either he used listen songs or went outside. He was wasting his time while others were study. And end result, second prelims he gets bad score.

One day

Anu didn't come to collage Pooja tells them she is not feeling well. Last lecture was off so Navin told her to stay for a while. They four sit in the canteen as there was free time. Ordered the coffee and random talking.

"Anu have anyone special friend?" Sham asked Pooja. Pooja rolled her eyes and share smile towards him.

"Why?" She asked.

"Just asking...." Sham said. "Is there anyone from collage or school?" He added. She stays silent for minute. As Sham think he asked something wrong.

"Sorry if I asked something wrong?" Sham said politely. Pooja was still looking at him.

"Tell him" Navin put his coffee cup on table and said to her. Pooja nodded and looked at Sham.

"Listen Sham... there is something out there... that really like ...a past." She was talking with lot of pauses.

"Few years ago, Anu cousin sister was in love with some guy from his collage. They completed their education and both get the steady jobs. They asked about them with her papa. But her papa refused as they wanted to arrange her marriage with their choice. So they ran away. Marry in court and start to live together. They were both happy with each other but it breaks her papa's heart.

They didn't talk with her. We were in school at that time. After that Anu decided that she will not do anything that makes her papa feels sad about her. She always listens to him and loved him more than anyone.

We had a lot of friends when we were in collage but she would keep distance with them. She does not have anyone like you asked but, believe me, she really likes you. I saw her. She talks with you so freely that she thinks you are his special friend. But don't tell or asked about it with her. And she really care you, she ask me when you were at home."

Pooja stop talking. Navin drink his coffee.

"Sham...?" Pooja asked as Sham was stunned. He was thinking deeply.

"He didn't listen" Navin moved from his seat and pat his hand on Shams hand. "She is asking something"

Navin went to get the coffee again.

"You liked her, Right" Pooja asked.

Navin came and sit; He gives the hot coffee to Sham and moved his previous coffee which was cold while listening.

"No, I mean....." Sham as he stumbles while talking.

"We all know how much you Adour her. She also knows. You used to notice her while lectures. And because of it you have to sit on first bench, all she knows. Just don't want to feel you bad" Pooja looked in her watch. It was around 5 PM something.

"I think I should go now, Will get late."

"Ok. Go safe." Navin said.

"Sham, Listen. You are really good and she likes you. You both are really good friends. Everything will happen at right time. Trust the process and don't rush for anything. Wait, whatever really great for you, will get at a perfect time. She understands you. Respect her."

"Bye, will meet you tomorrow." She adds in it and waves her hand. Starts his scooter and went.

Sham was in deep thoughts. Navin thinks that he should wait for some times. After some time, Sham looked at Navin.

Navin was feeling very bad as he found someone but Sham was struggling for it. Before he talks something Sham pick up his bag and said "Let's go."

Sham came at room. He was still numb. He went straight in shower. Removed his cloths and start the shower. The cold water made him little relaxed. He stands there for long time. Naked ...Thinking...

Someone knocked on door. "Is anyone inside?"

"I am"

"Ok, I think someone left shower on"

Sham comes out of bathroom. Wears cloths and went straight on bed. He fast asleep.

Sham was in sleep when Abhi calls him. He checked in mobile. There was 9 PM.

"Let's go for dinner." Abhi told him to get ready. Sham didn't say anything.

"You sleep early today?" Abhi again asked. Sham again didn't respond.

The all get ready. Went to mess. While eating, he gets call from Navin. He was outside of the mess. Sham finished his meal and came outside. Navin come to visit him.

"let's go for ride."

"No... not in mood." Sham said with lower tone.

"That's why I came." Navin said.

Sham sits on the backside of the bike. Navin start his bike they went to backside of the town. There was so much cold in air. He stops his bike. There was a small water cannel. They sit there for a long time. When Sham get its late, He told Navin to get back to room. Navin dropped him to room and then he went to his residence.

@Around 11 PM

Abhi came outside of the room. Sham was waiting for him. They went outside. Abhi smoked and they come together on room. Sham was trying hard to get sleep. Today he was not even in mood to listen music. He was just keeping changing his sleeping positions again and again. It was not working out. He checked on mobile. There was 12.30 AM.

He gets up. Drink cold water. Went to the balcony. He was looking something. He try look everywhere but didn't find it so get again on bed. It was Amavasya.

He sleeps for long time before so find difficult to sleep.

He opens the new book. Was reading till 2 AM. At that time he really thinks that he is tired. He lay his body on bed and closed his eyes. Because of the tiredness he sleeps.

Next day

Geevan was trying to get him up. Sham said to go he will come later. He sleeps for long time. When he gets up there was 10 AM. He still was in bed with open eyes. He was not in mood for going collage. When he gets hungry, get up, brush teeth, and went to snack center. Order the Poha and tea.

While he was eating, his mobile rings. It was Navin.

"Where are you?"

"Eating"

"Are you coming to collage or not?"

"I don't think so. Whole body has pain something"

"Ok, Rest."

"By the way, she also not came today. She is fine and taking rest. Will be came tomorrow."

"Hmmm"

"Fine, take care."

He comes to room. Again read book till the 3PM. He feels hungry. It was also late as the normal day. He again comes outside. Eat but don't want to go again at room. Instead he starts to walk on the road, where they use to go collage. Instead of turn, he goes straight. After a 5 min he saw, there was a park. He went inside it. There was no one there. Because it was too much far from highway and there was no societies around there. It was also small Park. But lots of trees. There were lots of flowers bushes there. Bougainville was all looking fresh among them. At the end there was small temple. Maybe because of the temple they increase the area to the park. He sits on bench. After some time and an old man came. He went to the temple, place red flowers and sit on the bench beside it. With shaking hand it take out something from pocket. He takes it in hand and spread in front.

Around 7-8 sparrow's comes in short and start to chirp and eat them, It was the rice or something white in color. When he finish, He gets up and starts to walk. He stops where Sham was sitting. He makes his hand forward. There was something in his hand. He wanted to give as 'Prasad.' It was puffed rice and sugar cubes. Sham takes it.

After a long time Sham think he should went to the room now. He checked his mobile. It was 4.30 PM. It was collage day time about to end. He gets up and starts to walk. In middle his phone rings. It was Navin.

"Where are you?"

"Wait, coming"

Sham hung up the call. And start to walk fast. They all were in the snack center drinking tea. Sham comes from the collage side road, Navin got confused.

"You were in collage?"

"No I went straight"

"Why"

"For the walk..."

"You could have come to canteen and sit there"

"I didn't want come to collage"

"Is everything ok?"

"Yeah, I feel pretty fresh now."

"Good"

They all had tea.

Next day

Collage day start. Anu came. Sham also came as he was feeling good. In mid recess everyone went outside to lunch. Sham didn't go. He still sits in classroom.

"You are not coming?" Anu saw him and asked.

"I am full." Sham fakes.

"Ok" Anu and Pooja didn't go. They sit beside another bench. Open their tiffin's. Anu asked him to join them. He refused.

"Pooja said, yesterday you were not feeling well." Anu asked while eating.

"Hmmm" He was looking outside of window.

"What happened?" Anu asked while eating

"Nothing just headache."

"You really want to eat? Mummy packed a lot and I cannot finish this" She was eating slowly.

"No its ok, I am not hungry"

"Fine" Anu said and packed her remaining tiffin.

Collage day ends.

They all come out of the classroom.

"Tea?" Sham asked as he thinks behaved with her little rough during eating.

"Ok" Anu said. And all they come in the canteen.

Sham sits beside the Anu. All he was noticing her. Her hair were coming on eyes, with one hand she adjust it behind the ear. After some time she place her cup on table and with both hands she tie her hairs with hairband.

Sham was looking at her. She was looking so precious.

"I think I really needed that tea. Feeling really fresh." Anu said while looking at Sham.

Sham smile. And finish his tea.

*12 September

She comes today. Looking tired And I behave bad... She asked me to eat with her and I say no. I think I did it wrong. So I asked tea after collage. She has a different earing today.

@Around 11PM

Sham was reading book. Abhi come, He calls him. It was first time Abhi asked him to come along. He surprised. Without speaking anything, he put bookmark on that page and closed it. Place it on table and gets up. Wear his hoodie.

They come out of the room. Start to walk. They came near the highway. Cross the road. Abhi finishes his cigarette. And they start to walk again. They didn't share any word till yet.

They came near the snack shop where they used to sit after the collage. It was closed. There were two benches outside. Abhi sit on the bench. Sham also sits beside him.

Everything was so silent that they can hear the vehicles running on highway which was far away. There was no one out there. Everyone was asleep.

"What happened?" Abhi breaks the silence.

Sham looked at him and as he wanted to show that he is OK, he nodded his head in nothing.

"Last two day, you are not OK. Feeling like low."

"No, I am ok" Sham said.

"Look, I know that I am not your best friend like Navin but I can feel that" Abhi placed his hand on his shoulder.

Sham stays silent on this.

"You asked her?" Abhi asked his again.

"No, I don't have feelings in that way with her." Sham laugh and told him as it was like nothing. He was hiding tears in his eyes.

"We all know that how much you like her."

"I think if I didn't ask will be better, May be we will be good friends" Sham said.

"It's on you."

"I think she is really good girl, If I asked her, it will be something different, maybe uncomfortable and May we could not talk after that as we talk now. And................" He stops. He checked his mobile there was 11.15 AM something? "We should go now."

Abhi did not get up he still was there. Sham calls him.

"What are you thinking?" Sham asked him.

"You are thinking how it will be possible? She has filled the form with open category and you SC category. Right?"

Abhi just explained in just whole in one line.

Sham stunned.

He never thinks this in that way till now. All he was thinking was not that deep. Now he was looking at Abhi with wide open eyes.

He gets the actual situation right there. He sits beside the Abhi.

"Look, whatever is going just let it in flow. Be her good friend. There are two more years right there. Don't make it fast. When you think it's perfect just ask her. Till don't be like this. These things are happencd. But don't feel bad about this. Be happy and spend good time together. Everything will be perfect at the end" Abhi said whatever in his mind. Sham was still thinking.

"Don't think too much about it. Be relaxed, you had not break-up yet. You can see her tomorrow." He said with keep his arm on his shoulder and cheers him.

"Yeah, you are right. I am thinking too much about it."

"See. Its 11.30 PM now, we really need to go sleep"

Both Sham and Abhi gets up. Sham was feeling good after talk. Abhi was really happy that he revises his mind.

They come in room. Abhi wash his hands and face and comes in balcony. Sham was there. Sky was clear. There was full moon. So much stars like infinity. Cold. Abhi went to his room.

Sham saw something. It was shooting star. He did not believe in this type of stories but still he closed his eyes. Mumble something. And open his eyes.

He was not feeling to sleep. He sits there. After some time he thinks it will be late he stays awake. So he comes on bed checked the mobile. It was 12.15 AM. He lay off his body on bed. Within a minuet he falls asleep.

He can see sea. Sky. He looked down. Water was passing through his legs. Someone calls him. He looked back. She was Anu. Sitting on bench, in classroom... Suddenly, again someone calls him. All disappeared.

"Sham.... Sham....?" Geevan who was sleeping his next bed was calling him.

"What happened" He was looking with half sleepy eyes. Sham still was confused. He looked beside. There was no sca, not classroom.

"You were calling someone; I thought for me.., maybe you were in dream. Sleep" Geevan goes to sleep again.

It was dream. He checked in mobile. It was 4 AM. Sham closed his eyes and was trying hard to sleep. He was trying to remember. All he can see *Anu was on the beach.*

Geevan was telling him to get up. Sham told him to go ahead; He will be there and sleep. He gets up. Check his mobile. It was 9.45 AM. Again late.

He gets ready and starts to walk towards the collage. He comes directly in the classroom. There was no one. May be recess was not end. Bell rings. Everyone comes in classroom. Seeing Sham sitting on first bench, Navin sit beside him.

"Wow, its first time you made it before us..." Anu tease him. And sit behind his bench. Sham just smile. Day ends. They all had tea at canteen, little talk and then went to home.

For the next month, they all were busy completing manuals, assignments. Time was passing either a lectures or the library. Everyone was busy in there. Sham was trying to be far from Anu. He used to talks with her little. Anu noticed it but didn't ask about this. Lots of time she used to ask him something. Sham would talk little and sit quite.

Orals exams completed. And then submission came. And then there was break for the first semester exam. They stay there and used to study whole day on room. In the evening Sham used to go in that park, One day Abhi came along with him. He like that place so much he insisted to go every morning there.

Day's passed and third semester ends. Everyone was studying hard to get good score. Sham was also studying but lot of time he used to listening songs or facebook. After the exams they again went Pune to Roam. After that they all go to their homes.

Sham comes home but he was feeling low. It was long holidays but still was not enjoying as he was previous before. All day he used to stay at home and watch TV or sleep. Navin would get to him and then he would go beach to play or the short trips.

Fourth semester

Fourth semester starts. They all used to attend the lectures and results declared. All gets good score except Sham. He failed in two subjects. Everyone was happy for themselves but because of Sham they didn't celebrate. Abhi was really feeling bad for him. But he was helpless.

In February Annual functions start. Everyone in collage was exited for that period. After all there was going to be fun in the collage beside the studies.

They all were participating in different competition, sports or whatever there different events were. Sham was not interested. So he decided to stay on room. But Navin call him and insist to come there. Also collage made the compulsion that everyone should participate in the events. So he thinks to participate. All this things were handling by the seniors and committee members.

First day -Technical Events day

There was lots of events arrange by the collage.

Project presentation, Paper presentation, Innovations Coding and Quiz and more. All the students were participating in something.

Sham and Navin named in the paper presentation. They made their presence in the at least participation certificate.

Geevan participated in the Innovations and he present his idea which was he working for the last 1 month and judges were impressed by his work. He got the silver medal for it. Sham and Navin were feeling so great that they decide to do next time something like him.

They all were sitting in backside of auditorium. Quiz was going to be in short time. Anu and Pooja named for quiz. Anu gets up. As she gets up, her sandal struck in the bench and it tear the belt.

"Shit ...." Anu said with the anger.

"What happened?" Sham who was sitting in front, asked her. Anu was standing with an upset face looking at her feet.

"Get your shoes?" Anu said while he removes her sandal's and slides both of them near Sham.

"Why?" Sham asked as he didn't get what happened.

"My sandal, torn his belt, Give me your shoes, Hurry." She said furiously as she was getting late. Buzzer was actually rang. Participating student were on the stage.

"Let's go" Pooja said and looked at the Anu.

"Just a Minute, Hurry Sham" She shouts on him again.

Sham gives her shoes. It was black sneakers. Anu was wearing formal white shirt with red tie and black pant. Wear the shoes. Start to walk.

Sham was looking at her. She was looking like the CEO of the company something. So much formal and dashing. Sham was just looking her. For the first time he feels butterflies in his stomach.

"Anu ..." Sham called her. Anu looked back. As she moves her hair comes in front of the face, she moved it with her hand.

"Best luck" Sham wishes her. "You Too Pooja"

"Thanks" Pooja said. Anu just smile.

They went towards. Quiz was going to be start and they stand on their positions. Buzzers range and quiz starts.

They were giving answers within seconds and they all were absolute right. Quiz was so tough but still they both managed it. Buzzer rings and they check for the score. Anu and Pooja had the maximum answers. They were in next round.

Department students cheers for them both. Sham was looking at her with smile. She smiles back. Both girls come and sit on the desk. Both were happy.

"Wow, you won." Navin congratulate Pooja for success.

"Not yet, there are another 2 rounds and then ..." Pooja said while resting herself on the back of the desk. Anu was drinking water.

"You will..." Sham said.

"These shoes are really lucky" Anu said while raised her eyebrow.

"No they are not actually, I wear them in exam and failed." Sham said cold voice. All start to laugh and Sham was the one who was not controlling his laugh on own joke.

"Maybe, lucky for me" Anu said and wink her eye.

Sham didn't say anything on the reaction.

Next two rounds completed and they won the first price. They all were happy and specially the Sham, because when the first round ends and she thinks that shoes were lucky for her, Sham just wish that they should not lose any round and won the quiz. He relived.

"Yeah we won, I said you, this shoes are lucky for me." Anu removed shoes and give it to Sham.

"Don't remove it, Navin went to room and brings the sandal." He said while showing his legs. He was wearing sandals.

"Your sandals" Sham give carry bag to her. Anu puts her sandal in the carry bag and then in collage bag.

"Let's go to canteen, Celebration time." Anu said happily.

They went to canteen. Anu throws the samosa party and coke. After a long time Sham was feeling fresh with that moment. All he was really happy for Anu.

Next day -Non-technical day

There were a lot of events that really excited for. There were games and the creative competition.

Treasure hunt, Poster design, Tech Photography, Tech meme competitions.

Sham was in sleep in his room. As he was okay with the one certification, he doesn't want to participate in another competition. His mobile rings.

"Where are you?" Navin shout on his phone.

"Don't be loud, I am Sleeping" Sham said while he changed his position.

"Anu is asking for you." Navin said.

"Why? She has my shoes." Sham said in sleepy voice.

"Not for your shoes idiot, just come to collage."

"Ok Coming." Sham gets up. Get ready and comes to the collage. Anu gives shoes to him. Sham wears it and placed his sandals in bag.

"For what, you were calling?" He asked to Navin.

"Look I won third in the poster making and added your name in photography and submitted some photos and this is your certificate." Navin gives him the certificate. He looked at it and said to him.

"Wow, without participation, I got it" Sham looked at the certificate and smile.

"Give me your shoes." Anu said when she comes and sit behind him.

"You have your Shoes." Sham said coldly.

"I want to win" She was pitching her voice.

"It was you, who win last day, not my shoes."

"I don't care, Only 15 min. Game is going to be start."

"She will not listen, give her." Navin said.

Sham removed his shoes and put his leg in her shoe. Her shoes size was shorter for him. She was looking at this and laughs. Sham chuckles.

"Just hold it" She said and Sham nodded his head.

Anu went to competition and comes with third number. She was not happy. Came with full of anger on his face. She sits two benches across the Sham.

"Every day you can't win its OK..." Sham said while returning her shoes. She was still sitting with folding hands.

"You didn't wish me." Anu said in sudden. Sham didn't get what to talk next.

"At least you won third, let's celebrate."

"Go and eat" She was still not happy.

"It's from me. Pleeeease.... Next time will wish you" Sham said. She looked at him and gave her best smile.

Everyone moved towards the canteen. Sham ordered the samosas and tea. Everyone was in good mood. They all were cherishing the moment.

Next day -Cultural events

There was a singing, dancing, debates, and social awareness programs. Sham and Navin were not interested in this but still were in collage because of the Anu and Pooja asked them to come. Geevan was sleeping peacefully as he didn't care about all this.

All were in canteen. Eating samosas and tea again.

"You looked alive for last two days." Anu said.

"What you mean?" Sham asked.

"I don't know, what's in your mind but last 2 months you were avoiding me something like. Don't do that again." Anu warned him. Sham didn't say anything. Finish his tea and all day they just roam in the campus.

Next day -Sports day

There was football and cricket match organized by the all department. They all five went to watch the game of cricket.

There was also the fashion type kind of events like twins day / Retro day / Mismatch day. They just think that they were on another planet. Some of them were so funny that Sham and Navin were making fun of them.

Next day –Suit and tie day / Saree day

"Where are you?" Sham picks up the call as he was in deep sleep. Navin calls him.

"On room, coming..." Sham answered in sleep.

"You know what day it is. Suits and tie day. Come with the collage blazer, don't forget. I am coming in 30 min." Navin reminds him.

"Ok" Sham said. And get up. Geevan was also in sleep. He awakes him. They both get ready. Pick up the blazer and start towards the collage.

They came in collage. Everyone was wearing suits and tie, Girls were in sarees. It was looking something like the fools business meeting out there on ground. They all were clicking selfies, some of them taking group photos and there were the girls who were making it like the beauty competition out there wearing so much makeup.

Sham looked at them and just wondering its looks like. Navin came behind. He was wearing suit.

"You didn't wear the blazer? I reminded you."

"It's in the bag." Sham said as he didn't wear that still.

"Wear it then" Navin said.

"Is it really needed to wear this?" He said as he was not interested to wear it because it becomes sweaty after some time.

"It's a suit day so enjoy it" Navin cleans his glasses with the Sham shirts and wear them.

Sham wears the blazer, while sudden Sham stop his eyes as he saw something special. Anu was coming towards them. She was wearing brown color, white strips design saree with the red blouse. She was looking gorgeous. Sham just lost while looking at her. She was in open style hairs. Her nose ring was shining in sunlight. Without makeup.

"How I am looking?" She asked as comes near them.

"Beautiful." Navin said.

"Thank you." Anu said in the pure melodic voice.

Anu looked at the Sham. He smiled.

"As always" Sham said while looking in his eyes. She wanted to tell something to him.

"Hey...smile...." Pooja clicks the picture of them.

They all start to take their pictures. They take lots of group selfies, solo, pairs. After that they went to canteen and sit there. Looking at the photos and finding the best of them.

"This one is best. We all five are in it." Navin said.

"Who clicked it.?' Sham asked as he doesn't get who actually click that picture. Everyone was looking each other.

"Mohit. One who sits with me" Geevan said.

"Tell thanks to him. It really a good pic." Navin said.

"I think this one is also good one." Pooja shows to Sham. It was candid pic before they were actually started to capturing the pictures. They both don't know that Pooja captured them both in camera before. They were looking in each eye's and expressions were natural.

"Yaa..."Sham told to Pooja.

"Show me." Anu said.

"I will forward you." Pooja forward the photo in mobile. Anu saw it and she blush. Sham notices it.

"It's really beautiful saree." Sham said while talking sip of tea. He was looking in her eyes.

"Yes it is. It's my Mom saree." Anu said proudly.

Next day -It was traditional day.

Sham and Geevan late again and were getting ready for collage. They enter in collage wearing white kurta and jeans. They came near the classroom. There was group of students. He can't identify the Navin. Boys were wearing white, saffron, red, blue and much more colors kurtas and girls were wearing beautiful colors saree. It was like marriage hall something.

"You look really handsome in this." It was Anu. She was wearing traditional green saree with same red blouse. She was looking typical Marathi girl. There was fake golden necklace around her neck.

"Thanks, you also look beautiful. Your mom has great taste in sarees." Sham looked at her saree and said.

"It's my choice." She said while moved her hair coming in front of her face. She always did that purposely maybe.

"It's really beautiful one." Sham said.

"Thank you" She said with melody.

They clicked some selfies, group photos and solo photos. After that they some spent some time in canteen. Drink tea and some snack and then they went to homes.

@Around 11 PM

Sham and Abhi went outside. Abhi smoked and then they returned. After that Abhi went to his room. Sham came in balcony. It was full moon. Stars were shining. He feels the silence. He stands there. Switch on his mobile and then start to look the photos they captured today. He was looking them generously.

He stopped. It was Anu solo picture. She was looking very pretty. It was candid pictures. The expression on her face was natural. He put his mobile aside. And sit there. He lost in the sky.

"I wish, I could tell her how I feel." One tear came from his eye and rolled down his cheek. He wipes his hand on face. After some time, he comes in his bed and closed his eyes.

He remembers when first time he saw her and then the couple of time he used to sit behind her, her smile while drinking coffee, and in the saree. Again he switches on his mobile. Looked at the pic and place the mobile aside. He was trying to sleeps.

After the annual function, lectures starts regularly. Sham has to sit in front still.

Sham was feeling great after the function. He used to talk with Anu properly. They get very friendly relationship.

Fourth semester was about to end. There were five subjects of them but Sham had 7 subjects to clear his academic year. He was stressed for it, also ashamed. Thinking if that time he would study May this not happens.

After the five exam papers, all relived, Except Sham. He had 2 extra subjects of previous Semester.

Anu used to came collage after the exams. She spends whole 4 days to explain him difficulties whatever Sham had. It makes him simpler to understand it in very short time. Sham also trying hard to clear his backlogs. After all Anu was spending his time for him. And also he wanted his mark sheet clean.

After exams, they went home. This time Sham was in good mood. He used to play cricket, football, spending time with friends and in evening he used to sit on the beach and remember the time when Anu was helping him for the exams. Navin also gave company to him.

Four days passed. Sham wanted to talk with her. He called. She didn't pick up the call. Sham waited. After a 10 min his mobile rings. It was her call.

"Hi" Anu said.

"Hi, Busy?" Sham asked.

"NO NO..., actually I was washing clothes, so hands were wets."

"With your hands?"

"No machine." No one talked after that.

"Sham..."

"Yeah..."

"Everything's ok?"

"Yes, I just... I feel.... to call you."

"Hmmm I am also feeling lazy. These days are so big."

"Yeah..."

"What you do when you get bored something?"

"Read books?"

"Suggest one"

"There something book name, I don't remember last time I was on Pune Station, I saw it. It's really has great reviews. I will text you in short."

"Ok"

"Where you will get it?"

"There is bookstore in here, I will ask there."

"Ok" Again no one talks.

"It's late; I think I should go now to home." As Sham don't get what to speak after that.

"Ok, Bye. Take care" ... "Bye" ....

Sham search on the Google. All he was remember the start something. He searches it and found it. He texted the book name to Anu. Holidays ends.

Fifth semester + Movie + Ajanta

New academic year started. Fifth semester start.

They used to attend the lectures and after that small talks in canteen and then they would go home. Days were passing. Sham and Anu were still there where it was. Navin and Pooja were now in relationship. They used to chatting, calling all time. Sham was not taking a chance to forward in their friendship.

One day evening when they were in canteen suddenly Anu leaned asked to Sham with little voice "let's watch the movie tomorrow." Sham surprised as he never think about it.

"Not in theatre, on laptop." Tomorrow will be Sunday and library will be open. We will sit there and watch the movie?" She told his like a secret plan. Sham was looking at her like she asked him serious question.

"What?" She asked as Sham didn't replies.

"Ok." Sham said after taking pause for seconds.

"Is there was any plan tomorrow?" Anu asked she think why he takes so much time.

"No, I will be there."

"Ok, Come at around 10AM. I will be in library."

"OK" Sham still was in surprised that it was a real or dream.

Next morning it was Sunday. On Sunday Sham used to get up at 12 and then bath and then eat. On this Sunday he gets up at 9 and get ready. Geevan get up as he thinks there was collage. Sham told him that "It's Sunday. I am going somewhere else."

Sham mobile rings. It was Anu. She asked him to come direct at canteen. She was hungry and wants to eats something.

Sham comes in canteen. She was there. He orders the Idli samber and they start to eat.

"What did you tell at the home?" Sham asked.

"Collage, with friends" She said while eating spoonful samber. That was delicious plate in whole canteen menu.

"On Sunday?" Sham asked with questionable face.

"They didn't ask so many questions." Anu said clearly and focused on the Idli.

"Good."

They finished their breakfast.

"Let's go. I don't want to miss the starting." Anu laugh as she thinks she cracked a joke. Sham was looking at her with slightly corner smile.

They came in the library. There were few students were doing their studies. They sit in the way no one can watch their screen and the can easily watch all over library. Both put on the headphones.

Movie start.

"It's English." Sham said nervously.

"So?" Anu asked surprisingly.

"On the subtitles, I don't get their words so fast."

"OK" Anu pressed the V Button on keyboard and start the subtitles.

They were watching a movie. Sometimes Sham used to pause movie to read some phrases. Somewhere in the interval Sham told her that it's really great movie.

"Yeah...." Anu said prominently.

"You watched it before?" Sham asked as she was so much sure about it.

"No" Anu said.

"How did you know then?" Sham looked at her and asked.

"Someone suggest me." Anu said. Sham didn't get it. He starts the movie again.

Movie was about to end. Sham was watching it very carefully. And movie ends. Sham feels like something watch unexpected.

"So how was the movie?" Anu asked while leaning her back on chair.

"It was good but may be they ended together will be good." Sham answered.

"Idiot. You told me to read it" Anu turn on him.

"What?" Sham get confused.

"That book, duffer, you don't get by the name. I thought you get that when I start the movie." They were fighting. Someone reminded them they are in library.

Sham starts the movie again.

'The fault in our stars.'

"It was the book, they made movie so fast." He was surprised on own.

"Here is the book" Anu pick out the book from bag and show him. Now Sham gets why she asked to watch movie.

"You don't read this yet?" She asked.

"Nope... I mean... I was about to buy next time. It was just I remember the name only." Sham said and lean back on his chair. For 2 minutes they didn't talk with each other.

"What you get from this movie." Anu asked.

After taking a long pause Sham said. "Be together till the last... And you?"

"I think we should appreciate little things in between us, Adour them, cherish them." Anu was looking in his eyes as Sham was also looking in her eyes.

"I think I should go now, Otherwise will be late for lunch." As Anu gets, more than 10 seconds they were just looking at each other eyes. Anu put his laptop in bag. And look at him. Sham was looking at the book which was on table.

"It will be anxious if you think more about it. Relax. Movie ends." Anu said and start to tie her hairs with hairband. Sham was looking at her.

"What, you don't want to go on room?" Anu asked as Sham was still looking at her.

They both came in canteen. Finish their coffee.

"Text me when you will reach"

"Ok" Anu start bike and went. Sham comes on the room. In hour Sham get text message that she reached home.

He sent 'Okay'. She sent again 'Okay'.

@At night,

Sham opens that book and search for that metaphor part. He writes it down on the dairy.

'You put the things that does not killing right between your teeth, But you never give it the power to kill it.'

You choose your behavior based on their metaphorical resonance.

And was thinking for long time about it. He was relating it so somewhere. He was thinking a lot of 'grenade' thing.

Days passed. They used to talk lots of freely after that.

One day Pooja and Anu both didn't come to collage. Sham feels like empty on that day. In evening they were in canteen. Navin called Pooja. No one pick up the call. They finish tea and about to go, Navin mobile rings. It was Pooja callback.

Navin picked up the calls and start to talk. His face became serious. He gave the mobile to the Sham.

"Haan , Pooja."

"Sham, Listen last day when we were going home, we had a small accident." Pooja said in quite tone.

"What and, you are telling this now, how are you and Anu?" Sham get freaked out.

"We both are OK now. She is taking rest."

"How did it happen?" He panicked.

"Actually when we were going home... it was rain so we stop for some time.... And then we again start the bike, There was pothole filled with water... I didn't get it and we fell off on the road. I was holding the steering but Anu loses me and she falls from bike and injured."

"Where"

"On the right hand but its ok now, There are minor scratches but she will be ok in three four days, Doctor said."

"Just tell me it is not that serious." Sham asked her as he worried about her.

"No, they are minor. Just slip the bike, nothing else."

"You really ok?"

"Last night we were resting after the bandages. And in morning think you will be in collage. Anu remind me five minutes ago.

"Where is she? I am calling her."

"I am at her home. Just a minutes..." Pooja gives mobile to Anu who was near her.

"Hello," Anu said with lower tone.

"Hey, are you fine?"

"Yeah, I am good."

"Tell me you are really fine."

"I am good. It was small accident, we just slipped.'

"Then why didn't you come today?"

"Doctor said to take bed rest and bandages so..."

"That's mean it not that small you talking"

"Don't worry about me. I will be okay in five six days. Ok...talk with Pooja."

Sham gives mobile to the Navin. They talk for some time and then hung up the call. Sham drinks the cold tea in single sip and they went outside.

At night Navin calls Sham. "Sham, Pooja said it will be great if we came to visit her tomorrow."

"At home ?" Sham surprised.

"Yeah" Navin said.

Sham thinks for a second and agreed with Pooja.

Next day Sham and Navin bunked their last sessions and went to the Pooja house. Pooja didn't get lots of injuries but there were scratches on her right hand. And then, with her they came at the Anu home.

Anu house was in same colony. It was small bungalow. Outside there was a garden. And a German shepherd was standing near stairs. As he saw them he starts to bark. Sham and Navin both scared. They backed. As he saw Pooja he stops to bark.

"What happened Rocky?" Someone calls for him from inside. It was familiar voice. She was Anu. She came out of the house to check who's there. Her hand wrapped with bandages and little scratches on face. She was not heavily injures but on her face anyone could tell that she was had bad accident.

As she saw three of them she just doesn't believe it. She was surprised. She just stood there for a while and smile. Looking at Pooja she said "You called them?"

"Yeah." While entering home Pooja nod.

Sham and Navin were still near the gate. Rocky was looking at them silently. Still they were standing there.

"Rocky" As she says that dog moved back and gets near her and stand beside her. They both get relived.

"Come in, He will not bite you, don't worry. He is good boy." As she says, that dog just little bark like he agreed with her. Anu pets on her back side of neck.

'Home Sweet Home' Written on door, it was Anu handwriting. English Calligraphy, often she used to write in notebook.

They sit on the sofa. She came with the water. Her mummy came with tea and her brother who was in another room just looked in the hall and then went to his room.

"You told me, there are not major's injuries." While taking sip of tea Sham asked.

"There are little injuries but bandages make it bigger." She laughs. All she was hiding her pain. She was messy. Maybe she didn't take bath that day. Hairs were looking dry. She was wearing pink loose t shirt and black track pant and flip flops. But still beautiful.

"Are you scared of him?" Pointing out at rocky she asked. "First time I saw you were playing with them." She said.

"When ?" Sham surprised.

"Behind the canteen, you used to play and talk with puppies"

Sham didn't get when he was playing with puppies behind the canteen. Suddenly He remembered. When Collage was start, it was first two three days, there was 5-6 puppies behind the canteen he used to feed them biscuits. But he stops when someone from canteen tells him not to feed them sweets things. They are bad for them, and they feed them the leftovers from dishes. Now Sham was thinking when Anu noticed it, at that time they even don't know each other.

"Sham..?" Anu asked him. Sham was lost for moment. As he gets after listen Anu is calling him.

"No I don't scare but we don't know that you own the dog and just came on us barking so... we..." Sham gives the explanation. He looked at rocky. In between, that dog walked and sit in front of the Sham.

Anu smile and said. "He likes you." Sham was looking at him and Rocky was looking at Sham.

"You wanted to take him with you?" Anu again said and laugh. For a small period of time she forgot the pain and was so much cheerful. Laughing out the heart.

"You never tell us you had dog?" Sham asked her.

"It's not mine. Its papa's. Right rocky" Anu said.

As he listen 'Rocky' he barks again and come near Anu. "Sweet boy" She pats on his neck.

They were talking, Laughing and finishes their snack. Rocky went to Sham and he started to pat him. Rocky feels good and then he started to be friendly with Sham.

After some time Anu's papa get home. They were wearing khaki dress. Sham gets confuse thinking RTO officers' wears only white dress. As they enters in home, share a big smile. Rocky who was seating near Sham, gets up and waves his tail and went near him.

"Hey my boy, There are guest?" As they pat him and asked. He barked. Sham and Navin both stand up.

"No need to formalities in home."

Sham and Navin both feel relaxed.

"How are you?" They looked at Anu and asked.

"Feeling better" Anu answered.

"I think we should leave, it will get us late to reach." Sham looked in watch and said.

"Please stay. She is feeling good. From last day she is in her bed. 'Rocky' play with them. I am just coming."

They went to get fresh. Sham gets little bit of anxious. Rocky came in front of him and waves his tail. Sham starts to tickle him.

"He understands everything what said?" Navin asked to Anu.

"Yeah, He is trained." Anu said as she was proud of him.

Anu was really feeling better. She was happy that they visit her. She was looking at Sham as he was patting his neck and talking with him like child.

"Still, in pain?" Anu papa said as they come and sit beside her.

"Not so much, Will be cover in short." and Anu wrapped her long skinny hand around their neck.

"Good, Don't moves it again and again. And take rest."

They start to talk about the study, collage and future plans. Sham and Navin were telling them. Anu's brother who was preparing for the civil exams joins them. They all were having a good time. Again tea gets served.

About an hour, Sham looked at the watch and think they will be really late. "I think we should really go now. Navin's didi will be waiting for him dinner."

They were about to leave. Anu dad wishes them for the future and tells them to go safely. Rocky was near them and still waving his tail. Sham and Navin sit on bike and waves his hand. Anu waves back and smile.

Navin start the bike and they were ready to go home.

"Her dad in RTO then why they wear the khaki, it should be white?" While returning Sham asked to the Navin.

"Will be on higher post" Navin said and asked "You scared?"

"No, Just asking" Conversation seems to be end.

@Around 10.30 PM

Sham mobile rings. It was Anu.

"Idiot, why don't you call or message me when you reached" She was furious, as she didn't get any message.

"Sorry, I forgot." As he really forgot when they reached and went directly to dinner.

"I was waiting for your message." She said with anger.

"Really sorry"

"It's ok."

"It been really late night I think you should rest."

"Yeah I was about to"

"Anu...?" he was about to asked something.

"Hann..."

"You tells me that your papa in RTO then... khaki dress? RTO officers wear the white, Right"

"They are on higher post so they have to wear the khaki. You scared of him?" Anu laugh.

"No, just got confused."

"Ok. Listen,"

Sham was listening. He didn't spoke any words.

"Are you listening?"

"Yeah, Talk"

"I... really feel glad ....that you ...visit today." Anu said that with having little gap between the words.

Sham feels good. As he didn't say anything she again asked.

"Are you really listing or in sleep?" She raised her voice.

"Just take rest." He chuckled on the phone.

"No really..."

"I was worried about you."

And hung up the call.

He text her. *'Get well soon'*.

He gets the message. *'Okay'*

He went out with Abhi at 11 and then gets to the sleep.

Ajanta

In between Department arranges the collage trip to Ajanta caves. Anu was not coming because of bed-rest so Pooja also refused. Except Sham, they all wanted to go there so they insist him come along with them. Sham also wanted to see the caves but he was not feeling good because Anu was not coming. At the end he agreed to come.

They all come at the Ajanta. It was rainy season so there was lots of greenery. It was really beautiful Curve. Lots of waterfalls ware making a noise out there. The Rivers were adding the music in this atmosphere. They feel calm and composed environment out there. They lost in paradise.

The all enters in the caves barefoot.

"This is excellence." Someone said.

It was the impressive artistry they ever seen in life. Finest work. It was so much perfection with only with the hammer and chisel that no one ever imagines. The paintings were impressive. The life of Buddha was exhibiting from it. Astonishing.

Beauty, Antiquity, Immensity, magnificent.

They all were walking. Looking at the sculptures, painting, and carving one by one.

"How can someone be so perfect?" Looking at the carving Sham said.

"If there will be mistake you can't tell that it's really mistake or just another piece of art." Navin said. "Really impressive."

Navin went ahead. Sham was still there. He was in front of the Buddha statue. His half-closed eyes were felt real. He feels like Buddha is looking at him. He was thinking something.

"I know it's really beautiful but there are lots of it, and we have to saw all of them." Navin said.

Sham looked at him. Smiles and moved to next part.

There were lots of artworks. Sham was observing all of them one by one. How can someone so skillful that carved centuries ago without any special tools or machinery.

Sham moved next. It was the long sculpture. It was reclining Buddha. He is lying on his right side, his head resting on the right elbow supporting his head with his hand.

Towards the Peace and infinity.

He was standing in front of the statue. Looking in his eyes. They blinked. That eyes made carved in the stone just closed and open in fraction of second.

Sham gets up. He was looking surrounds. There was nothing like it. He was in the room, sleeping. The entire city was in deep sleep. It's been 2 day after they visited Ajanta.

He checked his mobile. It was 5.00 in morning. He came in the kitchen, drink water. And then went to balcony. Sit there for some time and then went to sleep.

He was sure it was the dream. It felt so real.

Next day he ordered the same statue online which he saw yesterday in dream. It was made up of bronze. He put it on the books.

After taking bed rest and fully covered Anu come to collage. Ten days later Sham was seeing her. After the day ends they were in canteen they all were talking and drinking tea.

"So how was the visit?" Anu asked to Sham.

"It was so great that Sham think he is right there still" Navin said. Sham smile. Only he knows how was he reassembled it to his dream.

"Really?" Anu looked at him and said.

"Yes, there was great place out there. Caves, paintings"

"I just missed it" Anu said in nervous tone.

"We will go there someday." Sham said it in flow.

"When?" as Anu said, Sham gets uncomfortable. Anu also gets he get awkward on it.

Anu used to be in pain while writing due to injuries. It was submission time. She said to Pooja write it down for her. Sham said 'her handwriting is not that similar to her' and he will complete it. Pooja said 'as your own interest.' She handover all the assignments pages to him. It takes seven whole days to complete it. Anu did half of them being in pain. Sham tried to make his handwriting completely like her and all way he made it. He handover it to the Anu, But she didn't thank him,

Semester ends. Exams started.

This time Sham fully focused on the studies only. He didn't want to be like last time happened. He spends lot of time in library. If he has any difficulties he used to ask Navin or Anu about it and clear the doubt. He was not taking the risk at this time. Anu had also fully recovered before the exams. They all were preparing best for exams.

Exam ends. They all went to homes in holidays. This time Sham was not in stress. He was enjoying all the things at home. Use to talk freely. He shows photos of Ajanta visit to his family also the statue, he buys online. His papa tells him to buy the same to be in their home.

Sham and Navin used to meet everyday evening on beach and play football with their friends like previous and them sit on the beach till the sunset.

In between he used to calls Anu. Just to listen her voice.

Sixth semester + Movie

The next semester start. Again the annual functions came.

This time Sham was participate with full of dedication. He enters his name in the paper presentation and was runner up for it. They all three won bronze for the innovation. Lots of work was Geevan but Sham and Navin helps him a lot.

In Non-technical they participate in every event, didn't win any but at least they got participate certificate.

Anu and Pooja participate in Quiz. This time again, she wears the Sham shoes for luck and surprisingly they won again. She was so happy on that day. She gave party to all of them. Also enters in the paper presentation and get the participate certificate.

On the traditional day Anu wears dark blue saree. She was looking beautiful. Sham wears the same dress as last year. Plain white kurta and jeans.

When the day ends and they all were in canteen Sham tells said to Anu she looks elegant in blue. She blushed.

At night she sent the text message.

'You were looking as handsome as everyday'

Sham texted her *'Thanks'*.

@Around 11 PM

Sham just finished his Book, and waiting for Abhi. As he comes outside of his room they start to walk. They came at highway and them Abhi smoked.

While returning Sham asked. "Is it really helps?"

"What?" Abhi ask as he didn't get the question.

"Smoking cigarette" Navin didn't say anything. Sham gets that he never saw chatting with anyone or talking on phone in two years. It was like Abhi was smoking without any reason.

"Is it really something else or you just did it for to suffer yourself?" He asked.

"Let's go." Abhi said.

"Abhi there something is really killing you inside, this helping it more."

"That's not your problem." He increases walking speed. And they came near the room.

This semester years was his best year in terms of the all the things. He enjoys a lot in this year. He was having good grades in prelims. He feels relaxed. There was no stress about anything.

His relationship with Anu was friendly but he doesn't go beyond the line. Sometimes he used to show how she is important for him but never tell her. She knew that Sham is in love with her. She used talk with him freely. Sometimes she would share what's in her heart. Happy, sad, jokes, anger all she would expressed on him. Sham also handled her as per the mood very prominently. They were known to each other very well. Likes, dislikes, secrets too.

Sixth semester was about to end. Exams started. This semester too Sham studied really hard. All time he was in library and trying to get good grades. Exams end. After the last paper they all ware in canteen. They all were happy. Everyone was relaxed. They all had snacks and tea.

"Let's go for movie?" Navin asked while drinking tea.

"On laptop again?" Sham looked at Anu and said as he reminds her last time.

"There is new movie and everyone is talking about it. No is telling the end, But it's really great movie." Navin was telling the reviews of movie to them

Navin was talking about the movie named Sairat. (Hindi dubbed as Dhadak.) At that time it was house-full in theatre and praising for good storyline, Direction, Acting and music. Everyone agreed to him as they wanted to be relaxed after the exams. They think it would be a great idea.

"So its final, tomorrow we will go, Will you be there?" Navin asked looking at Anu and Pooja.

"Will tell you tonight" Pooja said.

"No problem, Morning there will be no rush and low price, I will gets the tickets." Navin said.

At night Pooja conformed they are coming.

Next morning Anu and Pooja came near the theatre. Sham and his roommates already were there. In morning Navin buys the tickets. They enter in the theatre. They all five sit in row. Anu and Pooja sit in the front row of them. As they didn't get the all 7 tickets of single line

Movie start.

The movie was actually shoots in village areas; it was looks like the Romantic-comedy movie. It was really entraining at all. Music was so catchy and perfectly written that everyone was really enjoying it. Some of the peoples were dancing in their seats too. Lots of whistles and appraising on the scenes.

Interval . Lights on.

Anu looked back. Sham and Navin were talking. She breaks their conversation and asked.

"How's the movie?"

"Good" Sham said. As he stop saying 'relatable'.

"Better than watching in laptop?" Anu tease him.

Sham smiles. And said "Nope"

Lights get off. Movie start.

Now it became the serious something. All the cheering, whistling stopped and everyone were tensed. As the movie forwards everyone was biting their nails as what will be happened next. They all get that the movies just turned upside down. Theatre became so silent. The background music was adding breathtaking experience.

Movie was about to end and everyone gets relaxed as the Hero and Heroine both started to live happy life. Some of them start to whistles like they won a war or something. They all think it was movie ending.

But still light didn't get on and movie still continued. In the next scene whatever happened in 2 minutes they just witness the horrifying experience ever seen in any movie. All the theatre was so much silent that if there someone drops the pin can make the noise.

They didn't even think about it the ending will be like this. Some of them were standing. No one will be there thinking that they will watch scene like this.

Movie ends. Light get on.

Anu looked back. Sham was still looking at the screen. His mouth was little bit open wide. He was like in shock. Everyone start to get out but he even didn't get up from his seat. While half of the theatre gets empty.

"Sham" Geevan calls for him. "Let's go, you want to watch it again?" He asked.

Sham gets up. They all came out of the theater. Peoples who would shout after the movie saying 'best movies, paisa wasool' were coming out with silently.

"What happened?" Anu ask as she think Sham was thinking too much about it.

"Nothing" Sham's tone was so silent that Anu gets that he didn't like the movie ending.

"I am hungry" Anu said. "Me too" Pooja said.

Everyone was hungry as they watch the movie in morning show and it was 1 PM around something. They enter in nearby hotel and order the Missal pav and Tea. On the TV that same movie song was playing.

Sham was seating beside the Anu. All they were eating. Everyone was discussing about the movie. Sham and Abhi were still silent. Anu looked at him he was not in mood of eating.

"Sham" She said so silent that Sham didn't listen it. She placed her hand on his hand. It was cold. Sham looked at her.

"What happened?" She asked.

"Nothing..." He said silently.

"This was too like that English movie. You get really emotional of this type of movies." She said. She was still having her hand on his hand and she holds it. She never did this like before. Her eyes were searching something in his eyes.

"No it's was not like that. But they could have another ending." Sham said.

"It was just a movie. It's a director's vision. Don't thinks about it so much. Finish it now. We have to go. It's been late." Anu distracts him and start to eats his meal.

They all finished their eating and went to their room. Anu and Pooja too reached at their home. Anu text Sham that they reached home.

All came to room. Sham feels like heavy head. He tries to sleeps. He was not feeling well. The climax scene was appearing in front of eyes again and again. He was trying to sleep. After some time he feels like headache. Eat the tablet and sleeps.

@Around 8.30 PM

All calls him for dinner. Sham gets up and get fresh. Along with them he went to the mess and had dinner. On TV the songs from that movie were playing. All they were enjoying it. Sham looked at the screen.

'They are having best time of love; they never imagine what is going to be in their life next.' Sham said to himself in mind.

@Around 11 PM

Abhi came out of his room. Sham pretending to be like sleeping. Abhi calls him and said to come along with him. They came outside and start to walk.

"You don't like the movie?" Abhi asked.

"What, No, I mean I like it. But it was little serious...." Sham said with little hollowness in voice.

"Yeah" Abhi agreed and stay silent.

They came at the highway. Cross it. Abhi gets the cigarette and start to smoke it. While Sham also go near the shop and asked something.

Abhi think Sham went to buy chocolate or candy something, He saw cigarette in his hand he run towards him.

"What are you doing?" Abhi grabbed the cigarette from his hand. And throw on ground.

"What?" Sham asked.

"Navin will kill me." Abhi threw his half cigarette down and crush it with leg.

"Who will tell him?"

"He asked me lots of times." Abhi said and grabbed his hand. Start to pull him.

"Lie then" Sham said disappointedly.

"Just walk" Abhi was in rage.

Abhi gets frightened as he thinks Sham lost his mind something. He thinks that Sham will never do this but he gets wrong. All he was thinking how to tell Navin.

The road was empty as always. Only two of them were walking. Abhi still was pulling his hand.

"What, You smoke then its ok. What will happen if I smoke it? Let me at least feel it" Sham said with the hideous smile.

"You should not do this; there is only one way there. It's hard to avoid it if you get that."

"I will managed it, Let me just have it."

"I am trying and didn't come out of it and you are saying will managed it. Listen, you will not come with me again at night." He leaves the Sham hand and they both start to walk.

They came near the Tea stall. There was a bench. Abhi went there and sit. He grabbed his head and was thinking deep. Sham sits beside him. They sit around five minutes there quietly.

"You said the movie was serious one but it's a reality." Abhi said with enduring nervousness in voice.

"What?" Sham asked.

"There are people who calls themselves educated but when it come to the point they show who are they real one." Sham was listening but didn't get that.

"People still are in narrow mindset in some topics. They didn't agree some things if they are not in favor, they just refuse to accept it. Some of them sort out, some of them finish out and the one who don't want to even tolerate this shit, **we try to avoid.**" He looked at Sham. When he said 'we' purposely said it loud and looked at Sham.

"You are in same boat." He looked at Sham and said.

Abhi start to sob. Sham was shocked seeing this. He never saw Abhi crying before like this. He used to think he was the strong one from them. He didn't get what to do next.

Abhi start tells something.

"There was a girl, when I was in diploma. She was from nearby town. When we were in collage, we used to be good friends. So we would be together lots of times. In practical's, Lectures, we used to roam in campus together and sit in library for the studies. There was nothing between us like relationship. Someone from her town tells his father about us wrong that I am getting with very close to her. And they asked about it to her. She tells truth but still they didn't believe it... And whoever told him tells dirty lies.

They managed to get my father's mobile number, told them to stay me away from her. My dad asked about it to me. I tell them there is nothing like this. We are just in same class. They just say 'stay away.' We managed to complete the collage without talking but you know..?"

Sham was listening very carefully.

"She was really good girl. Intelligent one. She used to like me and also I was in love with her. But we never tell to each other about it. I don't want to make it in fast. First

I wanted to build career and then I would have asked her. But they didn't even listen to us. And after diploma they married her with someone else."

Now Sham gets that Abhi is living with the utter pain inside him. Abhi stop sobbing and start to wipes his eyes with the sleeve of hoodie.

"You know what, the day when I get to know about Anu and you. I worried about you first. But you were so shy about her that, I get more relaxed about you. You even not taking chance. That's why I told you to don't rush, she likes you, complete the studies first and then ask her. And the best thing was there is no one-sided lover of her who will tell her father about you."

Now Sham gets all things clear.

"You know what's wrong out there; they still judge you by the surnames, caste, and religion. **They didn't look for who the real are you or your dreams.**"

"So, I will just advice you. **Be someone** and ask her father. Don't give a chance to reject you." All time Sham was just listening. He didn't even get time to speak something.

"You know what, we share the same surname, same religion but different cast." Abhi looked at Sham and laugh. That laugh was Abhi enduring smile. There was lot of pain on his heart. And still he was happy for whatever happened. It was killing him inside but he was hiding it.

They sit there for about 5 min there without talking.

"Let's go, it's late" Abhi looked at the watch and said.

They went to room and sleeps.

Late night, Sham gets up. He feels like someone called him. He went to the Abhi room. Abhi was sleeping.

Next day everyone went to their homes. Sham and Navin both came home. Again, family, old friends, cricket, football and sea. He was showing everything if fine but there in deep he was breaking. Whenever he saw that reference on TV, news, on Facebook post relate on that movie suddenly he reminds that scene and he would feel bad. And then used to go on the beach and sit there for long time. Sometimes he would call Navin to talk. Navin understood it.

Once Anu calls Sham but he didn't pick it. After some time he callback and talk, Say sorry for not picking up and then talk with her as usual. She tells him she is missing the collage. They came to back Pune in 15 days.

CHAPTER 7

Seventh semester

Collage start. Last year

Sham used to avoid talking with Anu. Whenever they would be together Sham didn't used to say any word. If she would ask something he just answered but didn't say anything after that. Anu gets it.

One day when there were last two lectures was off and the all were sitting in canteen.

"Why are behaving like this?" Anu asks him straight.

"What happened?" Sham act as normal.

"You tell me, what happened to you?" She was little annoyed. She was in bad mood.

"You always stay silent and didn't talk unless it's important. I don't know it's your attitude or something else you are showing." Sham didn't say anything. And start to walk.

"Where are you going?" She asks furiously. Sham just gives him the look of disappointment. And leave from there and went to reception.

After that Anu asked to Navin about it and Navin tells something fake that he has something medical problem at home but he didn't even tell him. Sham returned with cup of coffee. And sit two chairs aside. Anu sits beside him.

"Listen, Everyone in this world haves problems out there. If you think a lot about it, it may end wasting time on worrying about it. Your mummy and papa will take care about it and if needed you should go there and help them."

Sham didn't get what she was talking about. To avoid the more conversation he just shook his head.

Sham lean over Navin and ask about what she was talking about and he tells him lie about the family problem. Sham didn't say any word to him.

"Let's go somewhere, It will fresh your mind." Anu said.

"We have only 2 bikes" Geevan said.

"I know the place, we don't need bikes. And also Sham used to go there a lot..." Abhi said. Sham gave a look to Abhi. Abhi gets that he didn't like that idea.

"Where?" Anu asked.

"Let's go I will show you." Abhi said and get up.

"You are not coming?" Anu asked as only Sham was sitting on the chair.

"It's raining outside." Sham said as he was not in mood to go outside.

"Where?" Anu asked. Sham looked outside. There was no rain. He thinks for a second. And get up.

They start to walk. They reach at that park. Sham and Abhi went there after a long time. It was well maintained there. Due to rain there was fresh new grass. Lots of birds were there and all they were singing songs in their language.

Bougainville's pinks were spread across the park.

They all sit on the grass and start to talk. It was really mood changing environment there.

"You came here every day?" Anu asked.

"Not every day, in weeks, two three times." Sham answered. He was having 2 flowers sticks of Bougainville in his hand.

That old man who feeds the birds comes. He went in temple and comes out. He spread in fronts of the birds something. They all were watching him. While returning that old man looked at the Sham and smile. Sham also smiles back.

"You know him?" Anu asked curiously.

"No. Actually sometimes used to share prasad with me." Sham explained.

"That's nice. It's really beautiful place to sit peacefully. You didn't tell me ever." They spend there about half an hour and they start to return.

There was tea shop outside the park. Sham feels like low so he asked to them for tea.

"Not here." Anu said.

"Why?" Sham asked as he was craving for the tea. Anu showed him besides the tea shop. There were two boys smoking.

"I hate smokers." Anu said as he had problem something about it. Sham was looking at her.

"OK, when I was child, you know 9-10 something, I was outside at somewhere and beside me someone was smoking at shop. I get that smoke and feel so disgusted that I vomited there. After that whenever I looked at someone smoking I just hate them. They didn't think about the others." Anu explains him.

'Those who didn't think about themselves why will be thinking about others' Sham said in mind.

They all came I canteen again. Order tea and coffees.

After that they all went to their Room. Anu and Pooja went to their Home.

At night Sham used to go along with Abhi. Abhi told him not to come but still Sham keep walking distance with him. And also return in same pattern. Abhi scared that Sham will start to smoke. So he would go late, Sham still used to wait him and walk along with him.

In between Abhi was having his final year project work. But his project partners used to stay on another room. So Abhi used to work with them late and then come. He used to smoke while return. It will be late in 12.30 around. Sham will be in bed sleeping at that time.

He completed his work in week and then next day, when he came outside. Sham came with him. He thinks Sham was just giving him company as he didn't smoked yet so didn't say anything. They crossed road came near shop. Abhi gets the cigarette and went in the corner. As he finishes half, Sham also gives the money and came along with him with lighted cigarette. Abhi was looking at him. As Sham take puff of the cigarette. And he starts to cough.

Abhi gets angry on him, He threw his half smoked cigarette and comes near the Sham and hit in him on hand. Now His cigarette was in the dust.

"Don't do this." He said angrily.

"Why?"

"Don't be mad. Navin will kill us both and you know very well how she hates this." Abhi reminds him.

Sham didn't say anything. They start to walk return.

On next day

Abhi purposefully stay out of the room. At night he went to the shop. Sham was waiting there. Abhi gets the cigarette and start to smoke.

"You smoked?" Abhi takes drag and asked him.

"No" Sham with low tone.

"Then why are you here?" Abhi looked at him and asked.

"I was waiting for you."

Abhi finishes his cigarette and then they start to walk.

"You are taking this as joke."

"You think about it ever?" Sham counters.

"Don't waste yourself."

"What about you?" Sham again counters.

"You will regret it later."

Sham takes the long pause. And said heavily.

"I just don't know what to do." "If I behave good, there will be attachment and at the end, if it will not get accept, we will regret. If I behave bad then she will thinks I am doing this purposefully to hurt her." It was like Sham was had the written scripts.

"Just don't be idiot doing something wrong like this." Abhi said loud.

Sham laughed.

Next day.

After the collage day ends.

Everyone start to get their home. Navin said to Sham to stay as he has something to talk. Only Sham and Navin were in canteen. He clawed his nails in his deep in Sham's hand. There was blood start to coming from it.

"You smoked. What she will think as get this."

"Who will tell her?"

"I will."

"Tell her. I am not kid anymore."

"Wow, so you are grown up now to smoke"

"Yeah"

Navin stay quiet. After some time he leaves alone.

At night.

Sham and Abhi went outside.

"You tell him?" Sham asked his silently

"Yeah" Abhi answered. "And he is not talking with me after that." He added.

Sham smiles, Abhi didn't get that.

"Just tell me how many you had actually." Abhi asked.

"Two only. On that day and day before. By the way it's bitter in taste. And smells bad too. I don't know how people smoke it. And also it feels in chest like something burn."

Abhi looked at him and he get why he didn't touch it again.

On next day

Sham sits beside the Navin. He didn't talk with him all day. Sham stays quiet all day. Anu get that something is wrong between them but think they will solve in them, she should not interfere in them until necessary.

Till the semester end Sham and Navin didn't talk with each other. He also doesn't used to speak lot with Anu. Group became silent. If they would together all they just sit without talking. Anu thinks that Sham don't want to keep attachment much more so she also talk with him when needed.

Semester ends. Exam over.

They all studies very well so everybody was relaxed. Sham was worried for one subject. He gives its best.

They all went to their home. This Time Sham didn't go home. He stays at the room. He tells his home due to the project work he has to stay there. Navin went alone home.

Sham used to stay all day on room alone wasting his time on Facebook, internet and movies. His daily routine was just to eat, movies and walks to park. He used to read book late night.

Navin was not feeling good at home alone. He used to go on beach and sit there alone. He was missing Sham.

Holiday's ends.

CHAPTER 8

Last semester

They all came to room for the last semester.

Abhi came and get that Sham was all alone for 15 days he just get shocked. He asked about him what he did in his period. Sham just answered books and Movies.

Collage start. Last semester starts. Results were out.

Everyone gets good score. Sham was worrying for one subject gets good score. Now it was just last semester.

Sham was sitting on his first bench. Backside of him Anu was there. They were discussing about something. Navin came and sit beside Sham. He looked at him and smile. Sham smiles back. But they didn't talk with each other.

After collage sessions they sit in canteen. Abhi join them. Sham and Navin were talking together as normal. Abhi feels relaxed.

"Your mummy is angry for you because you stay here, And your papa were on me why didn't I stay with you. Only I know how I handled it." As they were talking freely like before and laughing, Anu feels good for both of them. After all they were talking after two months. She was looking at them, Pooja remind her to finish his meal.

Sham was coughing while talking. Anu asked him about it. He lied. Purifier is not working so it makes him sore throat. At that time Abhi confused because Purifier was working perfectly.

Annual Events starts.

Sham was working in committee of the department. He was member of the committee who was arranging the events in collage. They all participate in several events.

On the traditional day.

Everyone was there wearing traditional outfit. Boys were in saffron or white kurta and girls were in green saree as the theme was Maharastrian culture. Anu, Pooja, Navin, Geevan was there but not the Sham. Navin asked to Geevan where he is. Geevan said he went home last day by travels.

Navin calls him. Sham didn't pick up the call. After some time he calls back.

"You are at home..?" Navin asked.

"Yeah" Sham answered.

"Anything serious?" As he thinks something is wrong.

"No, mummi was worrying for me. There was next two days off so I think I should come here." Sham said.

Navin said OK and hung up the call.

After some time he gets message from Anu.

'It would have been better if you had stayed for a day.'

Sham made call for her. She didn't pick up.

He gets another message.

'Can't talk now. Call me later'

It was generated message.

Sham stay there for Saturday and on Sunday evening he traveled back to Pune.

When he came back no one was talking with him. He said 'sorry' to everyone but still they all were angry for his behavior.

Anu was not talking; even she was not looking at him. He said her 'sorry' and she gets more angry and said.

"You know what you missed?'

"I know, It was last year's functions, after this our collage life will be end." Sham said. Anu didn't said anything, she just walk out.

But later she starts to talk with him. She told them everything about the events, fun and lots of thing interestingly.

The whole semester was running fast. Lectures, Assignments, Practical's, Reports, Projects, Seminars and campus interviews. They were trying hard for that. And there was pool interview for the reputed company. They all gives interview for that and luckily they all four got selected for it. They hold that opportunity for the best because it was not the perfect but for the four of them were together and it also was reputed company. Also they were trying other interviews.

Now Sham used to go with Abhi to smoke. Abhi was feeling bad that he can't change for him. Navin stops asking him. But still he was angry for both of them. He was not talking with Abhi. Navin was known that Sham is getting frustrated without even in relationship. All he can do is to stay with him and support him for his best.

Projects, submissions, Oral exams completed. Academic year was about the end. There were only exams remaining of last semester. Collage committee arranges sendoff ceremony. Everyone was waiting for it. There was DJ music, Food, dance and fun. Everyone wanted to be there as it was the last function of the collage life. After all such rush, it was the celebration time for all the years they were studied there.

They were in canteen.

"You might plan to be at home again, Right?" Anu asked Sham with wicked smile.

They all were looking at the Sham. Sham feel humiliated.

"You will kill me this time." He said with laugh.

And no one laugh. Sham embarrassed.

CHAPTER 9

He asked

Function starts at 6 PM in evening.

Everyone came. They all were wearing western dress. They all were enjoying the function.

Sham wears white shirt, Jeans and a jacket which he buys last year but didn't use it till. Navin wear the half black jacket on his green shirt and jeans.

Music was laud. They all were dancing on music. Navin was also dancing. As Sham and Geevan can't dance they just stand in corner with some other guys and watching all of them dancing.

Anu was not still there. Sham was looking her for a long time. He was eagerly waiting. While talking with Geevan about something he suddenly saw.

Anu and Pooja enter in the hall. They both were wearing knee length dress. Anu was wearing all black and Pooja was in maroon. They were looking beautiful. He smiles with the corner of the mouth. Anu blushed. Sham raised his eyebrows and smiles as she is looking gorgeous. Anu mumbled in his lips 'thank you.' Sham gets that.

Music stops. They all sit in the arranged chairs. Ceremony starts. The department staff was giving lectures about the life and future. And everybody feels bored about it. They were not there for such things. After that some students starts to tell their experiences about the collage life, their experiences and how they enjoy in these years.

"Stop this crying and start the music, we are not here to listen all this." Someone from the back just shout. And the entire backside cheers for him.

They ended their two words and declared the sendoff ceremony is ended.

And the music starts. All the chairs get out of the hall. Hall gets clear in minute. Again they all start to dance. Were Enjoying their happy moments.

With group, solo they all were showing their dancing skills. Some of them were showing new dance step to others. Girls were also dancing by making groups.

Sham, Geevan and a group of the some boys were in corner watching them as they can't dance. Sham looked at the Anu. She was dancing in the group. Sham was staring at her. Navin came and grabbed his hand. He was insisting him to dance along with them. Sham said no as he know he will dance weird because he never dance before.

After 10 minutes, Sham came out of hall. He was thinking something. He came out of the building and sit at the bench which was in the lawn. He was looking at the mobile screen. In short time Anu came out of the building. She was looking for him. Geevan told her that Sham left 5 minutes ago.

She came near him. Sham looked up.

"What are you doing here?" She asked him politely.

"That vibrating sound is headache. Don't know how they dance on this."

"You are making excuses as you can't dance. Right ?" Anu ask and laugh.

He shook his head. Anu sits next to him. Sham put his mobile in pocket. They all were dancing celebrating inside and they two just sitting out there without talking.

"Let's walk for some time." Sham asked her.

Anu blinks as OK. They start to walk. It was night so there was no one in campus. The only sound of music was coming out of the hall.

They came near at another department building. Under the streetlight there were two benches. Anu went there walking slowly and sit as she was tired because of the dancing and feeling little pain in her legs. Sham sits on next bench.

There was no one out there, just two of them.

Sham was looking at her as she was sitting quietly. She looked at him. Sham smiles. And then from Anu's eyes tears just rolled down.

"Hey, what happens?" He came near and stand in front of her.

"When we going to talk on this seriously?" She starts to sob.

"Now its last day of collage and after this I don't know we will just meet again or not, and still you are not asking. Why you always so late. Just why you are doing like this? I am breaking" She start to sobbing fast.

Sham was looking at her. His eyes filled with the tears. He sits on the knees in front of her. She was still sitting on bench.

"I am afraid, ...and always was to ask you. I just don't want to hurt you." Sham said.as he wipes his tears with hand.

"For what?" Anu was staring in his eyes.

"Pooja told past things about your uncle and his daughter. And I didn't want that to happen to you because of me."

"You ever asked about it to me?" Anu asked.

Sham stays silent. He sits on the bench next to her.

"I Fall for you, when I see you at first time. It was when, I got scold for looking outside. I was looking at you. I just wanted to be with you. And..... that happened. I feel good. But when Pooja tells about all that, I just think to keep distance so we didn't get attach with each other.'"

Anu was looking at him. Listening him.

"You know, I saw you first time when you were playing with puppy's backside at canteen. For me it was first sight love something. When you were getting scold I got you that you are the one that, I notice. We became friends but never told you because I wanted to listen it from you. I was happy when Pooja told me that you have feeling for me. Navin told her. But you get so nervous that, at some time you would be nice and again sometime emotionless." Anu was talking looking down.

"You think we will be ended together?" Sham asked directly.

"When you came home to visit me. After that papa said to me that, you look nice guy. I tell him that you have feeling for me. They didn't say anything. But they are happy for you."

"On this traditional day, I was going to ask you but you were not there. And I feel bad. I just don't want to talk with you. But whenever I just look at you I forgot everything." Anu said and holds his hand.

"Will you wait for me?" Sham asked.

"Of course, I will." Anu said.

Sham gets up. He put his hand in his pocket. And take out something. It was ring. It was made up of silver.

"I know this is cheap. I wanted to keeps my 7th standard scholarship as my first reward but broke it for this." Sham said as he again sits on his knee. And show her ring.

He was proposing her.

Anu gets surprised. She didn't think about this before. She though Sham will never ask her.

"You matter. Not the ring" She said while sobbing.

"I Love you. Will you be mine?"

"I Will. I love you Too."

And Anu just hugged him. First time they were like this. Sham was so happy; tears were just roll down from his eyes in her hairs. He was holding her tightly.

They booth loose each other. Sham was looking at her. She was looking in his eyes. Sham moves his face close and kissed on her forehead. Anu feels like she was in dream. She kissed on his cheeks. They both giggled as they could not believe that it was happening.

Sham's mobile ring. It breaks their moment.

"Where are you both?" Navin asked.

"Coming." Sham said.

"Let's go." Anu said.

"Wait a minute."

He shows the ring that still was not gave her.

Anu forwards his hand. Sham put ring in her finger. Anu was looking at her proudly.

They both start to walk. Holding hands together.

They reached at the hall. Geevan, Navin and Pooja were waiting for them. Some of them were still dancing. There was rush in the dinner lounge. They five enter in lounge.

"Can we go outside to eat...There is a rush here" Sham asked looking at the huge groups of students there.

"Ok" Anu gets that.

Sham asked Navin his bike keys. They both came out of the college campus. and came near the highway. There was a small café. They enter in it. Sham orders the Burgers, fries and coke. They both start to eat. They were talking with each other.

Suddenly light went. Café worker came up with the candles and light it. Anu giggles as she never thinks it would be candle light dinner. She tells Sham about it. He smiles half. Café owner who was sitting at the reception was looking at them.

"Today, you really come with the ring?, Was so much confident." Anu looked at the ring and asked.

"I was in confusion that should I ask or not, that's why I was sitting outside. But then you came. I thought I should ask but still don't get how to start." Sham said.

Lights come. Anu was about to blows the candle. Sham insists her to not blow. The man sitting at the reception saw that and he turn off the lights, which was above them. Sham looked at him. He smiles. Sham said thank by expression.

"This is really beautiful." Looking at the ring Anu said. She was touching it with another finger.

"You like it?" Sham asked.

"I Love it." Anu said and holds his hand.

They were eating while talking. In collage Navin, Pooja and Geevan also finish their dinner. After that Navin calls him. Sham told him to come near the highway. Pooja was riding bike and Navin sits behind her. They came near the café where they were eating.

Pooja notice the rings and asked her about it. Anu blushed and said 'tomorrow'.

Sham told Navin that it's late and they should drop them at the home. Navin agreed.

Anu sits behind the Sham. Sham starts the bike.

Sham was speeding the bike. She was quiet. After some time, Anu places her head on his back. She wrapped her hand around him. She was feeling his heat inside her. She closed his eyes. Lots of thought were wandering in her mind.

Sham also feeling her. He was thinking is this a real or the dream something. He giggles as he thinking himself like hero of the film who is with heroin.

On another bike Pooja was riding her bike fast. And her hairs were in Navin eyes, mouth. He was shouting to ride slowly and all she was shouting I can't listen.

*'This, I feel never like before. We never get too much close this before. We both like each other and wish we will be together one day. I think I am dreaming but still, **this dream should never ends.** Not this road, not this ride. I just want to go on the ride which would never end.*

I am feeling great. I can feel it, I can feel alive, I can feel you.'

Sham moved his bike from Road. Anu opens her eyes. Pooja and Navin also stop beside them. Pooja was wearing her helmet. But Navin forgot it while leaving. As he do not used to ride on highway.

"What happened?" Anu asked as there was a lot time to reach home.

"Police" Sham answered.

"Helmet?" Police asked.

"Sorry sir." Sham said.

"You should wear helmets while riding" Police said. He looked at the Anu. And said. "It ok, Next time don't forgot. It's for your own safety."

"Yes sir" Sham said. And start to think how they just leave them without fine.

They reached at the home. Anu gets off from bike. Rocky came out of the home and put his paws on the grill of the compound door. Anu's papa was at the door.

"Just be here, I will came in 2 min." Anu went inside and came up with the something like dairy.

"Read it" She said.

"Your papa didn't ask why I am outside." He asked.

"I tell them. It was late night so you came along with me as safety." Anu answered.

"And about this" Sham again asked.

"I tell them it's yours." Anu laugh like a child "And it's really yours" She blush.

Sham also gives her a paper note something.

Anu waves his hand to 'bye' and went inside with rocky. Anu's papa smiles and also went inside.

Navin and Pooja came. Navin gets off from her bike. And then Pooja went to his home.

Navin take the charge of bike and Sham sit behind him. Navin start bike.

He was feeling the cold as Navin was speeding bike fast.

The both came at the room. It was 11PM something. Abhi was outside of the room waiting for Sham. Navin went to his flat. Sham starts walking with the Abhi.

"You proposed her?" Abhi asked.

"Yeah Finally." Sham said with crooked smile.

"What's she say?" Abhi asked again.

"She will wait for me." Sham looks at Abhi and said.

"Great." Abhi thumbs up.

They came near the highway, crossed the road, Abhi start to smoke. Sham was looking in his mobile.

"You are not smoking?"

"Not in mood"

"See, that how it makes to change" Abhi said. Sham just smile.

There was a message on his mobile for Anu.

'Message when you will reach.'

Sham reverts back.

'I am at room.' 'I love you'

And he was waiting for the message. His mobile beeped

'I love you too' 'Good night. TC'

'Good night. TC'

Abhi finishes his cigarette and they came to room.

Anu opens the paper note. It was letter. She starts to read it.

'Hey, I don't know how to talk with you about this that why writing this.

I am in really love with you. The moment saw you first, I think really like you. I love your face, your smile, your talk, the way you walk, your hairs, everything. You know it.

But every time just afraid to ask, thinking it will be mess. I don't want to lose you.

This is the last chance maybe that why I am writing this. I wanted to be with you. Will you wait for me till the time I will make me worthy to ask you forever?

I know this is not like the love letter but still if you think I made it just messages me 'Okay'.

Sorry again for making this again so late.'

Anu smiles, as she think if Sham ever writes a letter, it will be best one because all time he read the book, But he just writes it so rough. But whatever, He actually tried his best. She said.

She open her mobile and texted him.

'Okay.'

Sham was in balcony watching stars, texted her back.

'Okay.'

They both were in their beds. They hides their face in pillows and starts to sob. They were crying for the best.

They were kissing in the canteen. No one was there. Empty.

Sham gets up. He looked around him. He get that it was the dream. He looked in the watch. It was 5 in the morning.

He was trying hard to get sleep. He drinks cold water. It didn't help. He was just changing positions.

He checked his watch again. It was 6. As he reminds, Anu give something while leaving. He looked for it. It was on the table. He came in kitchen as Geevan was sleeping. If light gets on may his sleep disturbs.

It was card having photos.

Sham opens it.

He was looking at the pictures. The photos of Sham's, solo, some of them in pair and their groups. He was looking at them and remembering the time they all used to be together at collage.

At the last there was picture which captured on the traditional day. Under that was written 'Best pic of us.'

Someone open the door. Sham closed the card.

"Its last month of 3 years and you get up early. We should congratulate you in front of whole collage." He said sarcastically.

Sham laugh and said. "Don't tell anyone."

He replied. "I am going to tell everyone."

They all get up. Seeing Sham wakes up so early, everyone greeted him. They all get ready and went to college.

There were little formalities of academic were remaining. They were completing it. After that they all sits in collage canteen and were talking and laughing.

Anu was wearing ring. It was shining through her finger. Sham was looking at the finger. Anu smiles with half of her mouth.

Anu says to sit near next to her. Sham get up and sit beside her. He leaned over her as she was going to tell him something.

"Don't smoke. Ok?"

Sham looked at her and shook his head.

"Promise?" She was looking at him prominently.

"Yeah promise." Sham said deep voice.

Someone remind that Sham get up early today. They start to make fun of him. Anu looked at him and laughs. Sham also laughs.

"You didn't complete the sleep?" Anu asked.

"I had dream about you." He was going to tell her next but stopped himself. All he was looking at her. She was touching the ring again and again.

Semester ends. Exams ends.

They all get together in canteen and plan to go on dinner to celebrate it. 3 years completed. And the new inning of life was going to be start

CHAPTER 10

Her Dairy

5 August.

First day of collage. Heavy rain .We get late by half an hour.

When we were in canteen and eating, there was a guy talking with the puppies. He was looking so much funny. He was feeding the biscuits to them. I think he doesn't know.

I was in the lecture, looking outside. I think sir shout at me, but it was that guy. He was also looking outside. When sir was scolding him he was still looking at outside.

Bore day. In evening we went outside with rocky. Why he likes so much rain. There everywhere mud outside. I think I should tell him that too much biscuits are not good for the dogs.

10 August.

That guy is get late every day and get scold for not paying attention. After lecture he looked at me and smile. I don't know why I smile back.

Whatever I will tell him next time about the biscuits. But then he will ask 'When did you notice.' Forget it.

11 August.

We talked. His name is Sham. He lives near the beach. How it would be exiting to be lived near the sea. Whenever you just feel, you go there and sit as long as you want. He is lucky. Next time when I will saw him with that biscuits thing I will tell him.

13 August.

Now he has to sit on the first bench for whole semester. And His friend sits beside him saying he can't listen properly.

Good friends are always there for you.

16 August

He is geeky guy. I saw story book inside his bag and he forgets notebook.

He didn't feed puppies now.

17 August

He sent friend request on Facebook He likes my every photo.

5 September.

I think he likes me. Sometimes, he used to notice, I am sure.

30 September

Pooja was chatting with Navin. I asked him when we were in park. She tells me just syllabus talk. Who smiles while talking about the studies?

15 October

I am missing collage. It will be better at collage. TV is just boring. Pooja and I went to mall for shopping. She was saying Sham and Navin all day spent playing football on the beach. How it will be exiting to play there. I wish I could be born there.

30 October

Prelims Result out. Everyone get good score. We had a little party in canteen. Handshakes. He congratulates me for good score.

15 November.

He was looking in my eyes while talking.

13 December

I am missing collage again.

5 January

Results out and we all get good score. Sham failed in 2 subjects. Feeling bad for him. But he will cover it. He is intelligent.

25 January

I am not feeling well. It was like I covered it but during lectures I feel low. I think I should not have go to college.

After the collage Sham insist to drink tea. I feel better. He was looking at me while thinking something. His always have meaning less eyes.

2 February

He smile but I know he faked it. When he really smile, he look down first and then in eyes. Something bothering him. He avoids talking. He used to sit in library saying study. He think before says something.

20 February.

Today in quiz, we won. I wear Sham's shoes in emergency. But I think they were lucky to me. He laughs and said he failed with 2 subjects wearing it. Maybe you remove it while writing. When we won I saw at him, he was so much happy. But then he didn't show it. I threw a party.

21 February.

I asked him again for his shoes. He gives it, but we didn't win. He was right. 'You can't win every time' but still we got third price. I am happy. After the events he threw party for me and we celebrate.

24 February.

Pooja told me that she has told about the Simar and everything about her to Sham. And Sham loves me. I know that, he used to look in that way always.

I also like him. He is good guy. But not now, this is not the best time. He is going through bad grades and I also don't want to distract him more. Just don't ask for it Sham. Let be in flow like simpler in way. We will make it perfect later. For just now be good friend. I love you.

25 February.

He was looking so handsome in suit. He looks great in white shirt. He also tells me pretty. I got the best picture of us.

26 February.

He again wears the white. Was looking great. He should go to gym. He is little lean compared to other guys.

20 May.

Holidays are really bored. Five days are ok. Not more than that. He was sitting on beach and called me. How it would be beautiful, you are sitting on beach and the calling them. I crave to go there at least for one time.

He was telling thanks again and again for the help. But its and paradox like the shoes, you work hard that time that why you get good score. Not because of me.

21 May.

Feeling bored. He suggest me one book. 'Fault in out stars'.

29 May.

You really like this book? Gus died. I feel bad for Hazel.

31 May.

This Book is just pure.

10 July.

I found 'Fault in our stars' Online-Movie.

13 July.

I ask him two days ago will he watch movie together. He said ok. Today I showed him movie. First he didn't get that movie. At the end he said he didn't like the movie because of the end. Overall it was good. I tell him it's your recommend. He surprised. I showed him book.

3 September.

Today Sham and Navin came at the home. Pooja told them about the accident. He was playing with the rocky. After they go, papa tell me 'they are good guys.' I asked how you get that. They tell me Dogs can identify the nature of persons. They get, who the goods one are.

Seriously, I don't believe in this theory but they both are good guys. I know them.

4 September.

Last night I saw you in my dreams. You were next to me in classroom. Although we never sit together.

Bored all day. On the bed.

They are planning for Ajanta trip.

I called Sham as he was not going. I accidently tell him about dream. I don't know he listen or just say 'What'.

15 October.

I tell him I am okay still he writes down half of my assignments. He just wanted to thank for the last semester as he think I helped him.

17 October.

He is talking but not much more.

15 December

'I am missing him already.' It's been two days, holidays start.

17 December

He called me and asks me about the hand. It had been three month. I know you missing me but don't ask it.

2 January

He looked tired. I didn't ask him.

24 February.

This year again wears his shoes. Wins quiz again. He said I am intelligent that why.

26 February

I wear Blue saree as his favorite color. He liked it.

27 February

I purposely didn't tell him he looks good.

29 April.

I hate this year.

15 May.

We went to watch movie together. It was Marathi love story. Again Sham gets tensed due to the movie ending. Why he take so much serious about the movies. Its second time. He was quiet.

30 May

I think this year I should have been with him at his home. Don't know when I will be at beach. Ask papa for konkan trip. Busy.

15 June.

All come. Sham was in tension. Navin tells Family problem something

9 July.

We all went to the park out near the collage. It was beautifully cared. Sham goes there a lot I think.

15 July.

Navin told me Sham is smoking cigarettes. And he is not talking with him.

20 July

Abhi tell us Sham smoked just two. And he doesn't like it. Avoiding it. I will not also talk with him.

10 September

He sits in the library just doing nothing.

21 September

I am also not talking with him. Reality, we are not getting time in this scheduled like previous two years.

22 October.

It the worst semester I had.

Navin is not talking with him. He is not talking with me.

15 December

Pooja told me Sham is not with Navin. He is in room, here.

17 December

I called him. He says in is at home. Lied.

2 January.

He gets that he lie. He said sorry. I didn't look at him.

Navin was talking with him.

24 February

I am going to ask him.

25 February.

He is at his home. Fool.

28 February

Sham came. I didn't talk with him.

3 March

He say sorry for the traditional day. I was asking about the smoking.

4 April.

Fast running days.

26 April.

He proposed me with the ring. First, I was angry on him but he came up with the ring. It saved me. He asks to be with him. He asks me to be there for whole life. And I said yes. He was so happy, he kissed. I feel him.

After that we ate in candlelight. So romantic.

He dropped me at home. First time I was behind him on bike. It was so perfect that I just wanted to not end.

While leaving, he gives me letter. It was broken written but pure.

This is the best day ever.

CHAPTER 11

Corporate life Pune

Collage ends. Results were out. They got best scores. So got their appointments letter. Sham and Navin were selected for another company. Anu tells them to join there as it was good package. Geevan was also got selected for the company with higher package among them.

Abhi start to learn a design course. His classmates also got selected through the campus interview. They all leave the room with heavy heart. Before leaving they had a great party. They all were upset, 3 years they lived together as a family. With lots of up and down, but they never leave the room. Navin said them, they were the best five roommates ever had without living on their room. Navin also talk with Abhi and told him 'thank for being there for Sham when he was not there.' Abhi wishes him for better future. They all wish each other for best future.

Sham and Navin started to live nearby where their company was. They were so much happy that they were again with each other for the next. Navin gets his own bike and they used to go company. Anu and Pooja also used to go together.

They all were happy. Sham's and Navin's parents were also feels great that their sons achieve what they dreaming for.

They all start to work passionately

After the work they used to meet together at café and used to spend some happy time. Drinking tea and some snacks.

In the first salary Sham buys the watch for his father. It was square white dial black belt Titan and was very beautiful. And for his mom a handmade *Paithani* which was she dreaming from last few years. He courier those things as he didn't get the long leaves from office. Navin also buys the same and sent along with them.

Anu gives the first salary to his papa and they give half of it to get something that she likes. She buys the gold ring. And one day she gifted to the Sham. Sham gets overwhelms for that gift. He wears it.

They all used to go on long drives during the weekends, sometimes movies. They were spending their quality time together. On the Sunday night they used to go in restaurant...

Everything was great.

CHAPTER 12

Riot

Six months passed.

It was New Year. All were hoping that this year will be the great one. They all were making new resolutions and new target for New Year.

They all were sitting on the working desk. After the year-end party and welcome of 2018 they had morning speech about the new business year. They all were working. All were wishing everyone and happy for the New Year. It was the first day and of course everyone was ready to achieve more than last year. Some of them were thinking about their new resolutions.

All of sudden, the 5-6 peoples enters in the building. They all were having a flags on their shoulders. They were furious about something. No one was getting what is happening there, some of them were asking to another collogues what going on. They were confused about the situation around there.

Sham was looking at them. They were shouting loudly and he listen 'just stop the work and go home, there will no one work here, it's a curfew.' It was like he is minister.

Someone who was listening them, look outside by the glass window "Look what they are doing."

On the road there was mob, having a specific color flag were on their shoulders, they all were shouting. Giving's slogans, pelting stones. It was horrific atmosphere there.

The managers were talking with them in English and they were not getting that.

"Look, I just can't stop them to working." He hold his both hand together and was telling them.

"Just shutter down and go home, no need to work." He shouts and guys behind them cheers for him.

"I have to talk with the higher authority for this."

"Talk with them and just get the off the building, nothing else." He said and chews tobacco in his mouth.

Someone come, it was from their group and wearing white kurta and jeans. Maybe he was their leader or something of them. He came near the manager. Manager was still trying to contacting the higher authority.

"What happened?" White dress guy ask.

"They are not picking call maybe in meeting or something." Manager said helplessly.

"Look man, we don't have any problem with your personal, its whole state curfew. There are some thing working out there and you also cooperate with us. Just stop the work and go home." He said politely.

This was the third time manager was listening stop the work and go home. But 'why?' he didn't get that. 'What will happen if they work there?' He was thinking in his mind.

"Are you listening?" He shouts. This time he was furious by voice.

"OK OK." Manager was now stressed. "I will tell them to go home"

He said politely 'thank you' and then they all went.

Everyone was frightened. They all make a group where everyone was talking with each other and no one was getting what the other one is talking

Manager comes and said to stay silent. He said to make a little conference something. They made round and he stand in front of them.

"Look I don't know what's going on there outside. But they are saying it worse. There were 5-6 people you looked were saying not to work. I talked with the authority and they say that work in silent and don't let them get that we are working, just don't show. So closed the windows and lower some light and work silently. I am closing the doors for safety. If something happen moved towards the conference room."

They all come to their desk to work. They start to work.

Half an hour later, there was tea break so everyone gets their cups and sit on their chairs. Some of them were talking with collogues.

Sham and Navin were talking about what will be situation out there. They looked at outside. There was no one road. One police van just came fast and disappears at that speed. The siren was so loud that everyone started to look outside through the glass. They gets something is serious going on out there.

"Look what your brothers doing out there." Some guy looked at next another guy and said.

"What?"

"Your brothers, they are one who did the disaster out there. They are destroying public property and telling people not to work." While saying he looked at the Sham. Sham gets what he was talking about.

"Look man, I am out of this." The guy said and went to his desk. The first guy was still looking at the Sham. Navin grabbed Sham hand and pull towards his chair.

Sham was working on his desktop. He looked up, that first guy was looking at him, furiously. Sham thinks he should not look at him, he changes his seating position and sits in the way he cannot see his face.

Sometime later, it makes horrible sound something like breaking glass. It was so loud that some girls start to scream at the same time. Everyone frightened out. Three four guys enters in the office breaking main glass door. They all run towards the conference room. Manager came forward and start to talk with them, They were talking in slang language and just break the front glass door and was about to break another glass. Manager was consoling them.

They all were in conference room. Frightened.

Manager talks with them. And they went. Manager switches off the lights, and came in the conference room.

"Look the guys again came, not the same one. Their flags were different this time. But still they also said not to work and cooperate. Talk with lot of disrespect. I will talk with the authority and will be there. Just saved whatever you work and be here "

They all run towards their desk and then went to conference room. Manager was talking with managements.

Sham was looking at the first guy. He was trying to not look at the Sham. Another direction, the second guy was also looking at him. He feels humiliate.

"What are you looking at me like this? I am not the one who is doing this." He should with full voice. Everyone was looking at him as why he is shouting.

One guy who was the 5-6 years older than them was carefully watching all of their drama silently said.

"Then who are they?"

"How do I know?" first guy said furiously.

"But few time ago you identifies as that his brothers were there" He point towards the second guy.

He quiets. Just don't have the words against him. First he was wrong and second the guy was strong.

"Why you are not there with them having flag on shoulder?" He asked him silently.

"Why should I go there, I don't want lose job." First guy said.

"Why he is not doing that" He points out at the second guy who was sitting silently.

"How do I know?"

"Because he don't want to. He also don't want to lose job and just do like this"

"Hey why are you not out there?" That coolest guy point out at the Sham and ask. Everyone was frightened and that guy was asking questions making again situation harden.

"My idols didn't say this to do." Sham said.

"What your idols said?"

"Educate"

All the conference room became silent.

After sometime, manager came.

"Management said to stop work and go home, if possible work from home. It's not safe out here."

Sham and Navin came to the room after that.

Sham calls Anu, She faced the same situation.

The next three days were disastrous.

But this change a lot in his mind again lot of things. That there are some people who just want to see city burn while actually didn't even light matchstick.

In this period Sham start to smoke. Navin didn't insist him. He knows how Sham was feeling. He was the weakest guy about the controlling emotion. Navin told about this to Anu. Anu fights with Sham and stop calling him. After some time Sham said 'sorry' and said he will not smoke but He continued and told Navin not to speak about this to her.

CHAPTER 13

Bangalore

After a year, Sham and Navin asked to shift Bangalore. They didn't want to go there as this was the perfect 'work and life' balance. But it was reputed company to work and they were having good salary so they agreed to go there. Company provides all facilities to them. They easily get adjust there.

But Anu became sad after that, Pooja also as Navin was not there. They were missing them every day.

Anu used to call Sham a lot. They used to video calls. Anu always wishes to meet him.

Here Sham and Navin used to roam the city but after some time, they both get bored and they also start to spend the weekend in the room. Doing nothing.

Days were passing fast. Sham and Navin both were not feeling good there. But still somehow they would manage to pass the day. Sham became quiet. He used to go office with Navin and then come to room and sleeps. Navin at least calls to Pooja but sometimes Sham would avoids the calls and tell Anu that he is tired. Anu was feeling bad at that time.

CHAPTER 14

5 Days in Pune

After the three months. They both get the whole week leave. They came in Pune and stay at the friend's room.

On the first day they four meet in the café and Anu didn't even say hello. She was angry. Sham say 'sorry' But still she was not in good mood.

Anu gets Sham's bag and start to find something. As she gets the packet of cigarette in it, she asked about it.

"What is this? You told me?" She was furious.

"Why you are behaving like this?" Sham asked.

"Why are you doing this?" Anu points on Sham.

"Leave it, just eat something" Sham said silently.

Everyone in café was looking at them. Sham gets the packet and put in his pants pocket. Navin and Pooja were looking at them with disappointment. They were thinking, it will be good to meet after long time and they are just fighting with each other.

Anu was about to go outside. Sham grabbed her hand and said. "Look there is only five day here. And we get two hours and you are doing like this."

Anu didn't listen and leave. She went outside and stand near the bike. Sham calls her but still she didn't came inside. They finished their meal without her and came outside. Anu leaves without telling him bye. They didn't talk on that day.

On next day

Sham and Navin went out with their friends. When Anu and Pooja complete their working hours, Pooja calls them and said come to the café.

Sham and Navin came. Anu sits beside Sham and was quiet. There were tears in his eyes. He looked at him. Anu said sorry to him for last day. Sham was in tension because he didn't take out the packet of cigarette from his bag.

Two hours only they were talking with each other, Sham was telling her all about the Bangalore and she was listening to him. Navin and Pooja were looking at them and feel good that they were having the best time.

While leaving, Sham said 'sorry' to her. Anu didn't say anything. She just smiles. "I don't want the ruin next three days. Tomorrow I am taking leave, let's go somewhere together." She asked.

On next day

They made plan for Lavasa. Rain and chilling air was giving thrills while riding. It was beautiful atmosphere there. They reached at there.

"Listen, I talk with papa about us." Anu said while holding his hand.

"What did they say?"

"They don't have any problem about us."

"That's really great then."

"Yeah, I know but…"

When she said 'but…'. Sham feels like something is bothering her. He looked at her and groped her hand.

"My aunt have seen someone from same field, you know relative, how to interfere in another ones marriages, same like that. She is telling me to marry her choice. I tell them, I am not ready for this right now, And then she talk with my father. Papa said that 'I will do it in her own way so..'."

"So?"

"What so. At the end we will not have any problem in us. Just don't get stress too much about us." She said and spread smile all way across the face. Sham didn't say anything. He holds her hand tightly.

"Will you came tomorrow at dinner, I will cook" While leaving Anu asked. Sham agreed. "Navin, You Too"

"Ok" Navin said.

Next day

Anu and Pooja completed their work and then meet them at the café. They had tea and snack together and then leave.

At night Sham and Navin came to the Anu home. 'Rocky' welcomes him. He still reminds him. Sham start to tickle him and he likes it.

Pooja also join them. She helps her to cook and serve. They all start to eat. Anu's papa was asking them about the work, Workplace, Bangalore and lot more. Sham was telling them everything with detailed. They ask them when they will be here again. Sham said they also don't know about this.

They all finish their meal. Sham tells Anu that Food was great. Specially Paneer.

On next day

It was their last day. They were leaving that night for Bangalore.

Anu said they are going to Dagadusheth temple. Sham reminds that he can buy the books out there. They came near ABC chauk. This time Sham buys all new books. And then they came near the Dagadusheth. There was crowd in temple so Anu said will prey from outside. Sham says 'ok.'

They stand across the road. Anu holds her hand in praying. When she was about to close her eyes, looked at Sham, he was standing. She pokes him. Sham closed his eyes. They both were talking in their minds.

Anu give her the new watch which she buys for him, and Sham gives the gold ring.

Sham and Navin came to Bangalore. They were feeling fresh after coming from the Pune. Sham used to read whenever he feels low. It was feeling so good reading new books; He used to smell all time while reading it. Anu was happy as Sham was calling her and talking nice in that time.

Days were passing fast.

It's been five month Sham and Navin didn't go home, so they planned for it. It was Diwali, there were six days holidays. Sham asked Anu to come along. Anu asked at home, they say 'ok', she gets happy. Pooja also join her.

Sham and Navin first came pune and then along with Anu and Pooja by train. They all came at home. Sham gets Anu first time at home. He was feeling nervous.

CHAPTER 15

Konkan

Guhagar , Ratnagiri (Konkan)

Sham's home, it was old fashion red rocks (Laterite) home. Maybe his grandpa builds it. That was big. There were around 7-8 rooms maybe with huge kitchen there. At the backside, there was big garden. There were tall coconut, banana, mango, jackfruits trees. There was so much flowers plant in there Sham was telling her each name of it.

They were living in joint family home. Sham's uncle, aunt and their two children were also there. They were in school. Sham uncle used to run kirana store.

Anu likes the fish curry and rice. She likes it so much, she asks again. For the first time she felt it so much tasty. Sham tells her, because its fresh, not preserved.

After eating and little nap time, they came at the sea. She came on the sea before, but it was no like - you complete sleep and just get up and there. She was feeling jealous for him.

They sit on the shore. She was feeling calm. Was Listening waves of the sea. She forgot everything about anything she had outside. She just lost looking at the sea and his wavy noise. She was still in that moment didn't get that Sham was calling her. Sham poked her with the finger.

"What happened, you are not even listing to me."

"No I am listening."

"What did I say?" Anu gets blank. Sham laugh.

"Where you lost?"

"Nothing." She smiles. Sham get that she was lost in thoughts.

"You want to eat something?"

"No I am full, that fish really so much tasty, I eat double." She put her hand on stomach and said.

Sham again laughs. Anu was looking at him. He was in moment. His laugh was so real, Anu get that Sham hardly laughs like this. He was really in good mood.

"No I mean bhel or something, I mean you are on beach and didn't eat bhel, and you miss the real fun out there." Sham explained why he asked.

"Ok." Anu said.

Sham went and come up with the one cone of bhel.

"Just one?" Anu asked surprisingly.

"You said you are not hungry." Sham sits and gives it to her. "Also we can eat like couple." Sham blinked his eyes. Anu smiles. They were eating one by one, passing it.

Navin and Pooja came. After eating at Sham home, Pooja went to the Navin's home.

"Just married or?" Pooja asked as they were sharing same cone of bhel. And Pooja and Navin sit beside them.

"Yeah, like... look what if we had our marriage on this sand." Anu smiles and looked at the Sham.

"Look at them; they are here to watch on the people who misbehave here. If we had marriage here, may be that night we will be in jail." Sham points on random office building and then blink his eye looking at the Navin.

"Yeah one time one couple kissed here publicly and people beat them." Navin adds another lie.

"Ok. We will not marry on the beach." Sham and Navin laugh so hard that Anu gets that they were making fun of her.

"Why can't we marry here?"

"Then everybody will arrange here only and it will make chaos here" Sham explained. It makes Anu sad.

"Don't worry, we will keep reception here." Sham said.

"Really" Anu gets excited.

"Yeah... Of bhel..." Navin said and they again start to make fun of her.

Anu gets angry. But she gets that they both gets so relax minded that they are actually laughing with their hearts. Pooja was also laughing. She also laughs. All four they were just forgot all the outside and were cherishing the time.

Sometimes later Sham and Navin friends came. They call for him. They were giggling. Someone from them shout. "Why you didn't invite us on your wedding, Sham?"

Sham looked at them and just waves his hand. He tells then to go, play and leave them alone. They get that. After all, they were just teasing them.

It was late evening. They all four were sitting there. Anu feels so alive there. She was just wanted to be there like forever. For the first time she was on beach for so long time and she watch full sun was going under the sea. She felt it so much relaxing.

After some time they come home. And again different fish curry. She likes that too.

At night, she was about to sleep. But the sound of tides making noise and she can't just sleeps. She calls for Pooja. She was also awake. She message Sham who was on mobile surfing Facebook. He gave them cotton balls. Both girls get that it's not all that fun living there.

On next day

Anu gets up. Sham was brushing teeth in backside garden. She went there. Sham gives her toothpaste and they start to brush. Anu was all grown up in city. She feels awkward but enjoyed it.

Sham planned for the short visit. First they visit the Vyadeswar (Shiv) temple and then, Hedvi (Ganesh) Temple. At the noon they came at home and then at evening they went to beach again.

On next day

They planned for the Dapoli.

They returned afternoon. It was heavy heat outside. They all were exhausted by it. They eat and sleep. Anu was sleeping in the Sham's bed in another room. Sham entered in the room. Look at her face. She all was looking unfairly beautiful. Her flawless white face was looking like child.

He shut the half door but didn't lock it. He don't know why, lay beside her. His eyes were wide open looking at the roof. She was in deep sleeps because of tired. She changed her side. Nudge her head on his shoulder.

Sham gets horror struck. As they only two were in that room, if someone will find them he may get into mortifying situation. But still he was felling relaxed first time as this. Her hand was on his chest.

She gets something wrongs. Break her sleep. Open her eyes. For the second she thinks like dreaming. Sham was looking at her with little curvy smile. She gets relaxed. She closed her eyes. She was listening his heart.

All she was remembering the day when she was sitting behind him on bike. That same feeling but more euphoria. Ecstasy.

She opened her eyes. Look into his eyes. He was also looking in her eyes. He leaned lips towards her and kissed on her head.

One of the kids shouts on another outside. They both in spur of the moments get up from the bed. And sit. They both giggle for the moment.

On next day

Anu and Pooja were eating fish third time in single week. Sham mother said Sham loves to eat fish. When he stays away from home he didn't get that, that why.

All day Anu and Sham's mother was talking with each other. Sham mother was telling her about him and asking about her. Sham sister showed her their photo album. She was watching his memoires. At night Anu cooks food. They all like it. She was happy.

Late night Sham, Anu and Pooja went to beach. Navin joins them.

Sham and Anu was sitting on the beach. He looked at her. Dim light of the moon was spread in the sky. In that, her face was glowing. He holds her right hand to her left hand. She looked at him. That was quick. She laughs. Sham was nervous.

He leaned in and tilted his head to her side. They were kissing with oath of the sea, with waves, with the moon.

"Listen..." Anu looked at him. "I think it would take another 2-3 year's maybe." He continued.

"No problem." She said.

"Sad?"

"No, of course not."

"Once I will think it would be okay, we will do it."

"I will wait till" Anu said and places his hand around her shoulder. Sham feels better.

He looked at back. Navin and Pooja were also kissing.

Next day

Leaves over. They packed. And start their journey.

Anu like those 5 days so much she would never forgets. She lived there as like paradise. She likes that place. Especially the sea, she was never going to forgot.

After that Sham and Navin went to Pune. They dropped girls at the home and then returned to the Bangalore.

They feel better after that home visit.

CHAPTER 16

Again Bangalore

One day, Sham mobile rings. It was Abhi. Sham picks up the call. Navin was there too. Sham puts mobile on speaker.

"Hey how are you guys?" He was talking in full josh.

"We are fine, what about you?" Sham said.

"Still, in Pune. Everything fine, I saw your pictures, you were in Bangalore."

"Yeah still in here. They sent us here for six months. And still we are here." Navin said.

"And when are you coming here?"

"God knows." Navin said.

"You were in design right then?" Sham asked.

"One year internship and then they keep me here, not permanent but still Ok..."

"Nice" Sham said.

They start to talk random things and then,

"Listen, you both have to come on next month for marriage ceremony." Abhi told the reason of the call.

"So early" Sham asked.

"Yeah, I was working here and then there was a girl working here from my neighbor hometown. As time passes we became good friends and six months ago she lost her dad. Her family was looking for her marriage. She told their family about me and they agreed. They knew me. So we are marrying in next month."

"We will be there." Navin said.

"And... What about the cigarettes?" Sham asked.

"I stop it. I had chest pain due to that so... I quit years ago. What about you?

"Tell him, He is not listening both of us." Navin said.

"Look Sham, I distract that thing when I was seriously in pain; don't do that it will not help but just damage you."

"I will try." Sham uttered.

They start to talk on others things. They both agreed to come at his wedding. Their calls last long for hours and then hung up.

Sham was really happy for him. When he was in pain Sham was there, and now he was all recovering up. He feels great for him. And also that al last everything will be great.

*"*Navin...Navin...Navin...*"

Sham was shouting.

Navin was there on another bed but he was not listening it.

He was trying hard to move his hand, but they were not moving. He can't feel his legs; it was like he was only feeling his soul. He starts to push by his all limit but still it doesn't help. He starts to shout again. "Navin...Navin..." Everything was there as the room just he was not moving from his place.

All of sudden he open his eyes. He was in full of sweat. He moved his hand and swells sweat on his head.

Navin was sleeping beside peacefully.

Sham gets in kitchen. Wash his face. He drinks water.

He didn't get what was really happen.

One year complete in Bangalore and then they got call from Pune.

All of them were really happy. Anu went to the temple at that day when he gets the news; it was like she asked for it to the god. Sham was scared because of his cigarette habit. From last six months he was telling her that he was not smoking. But also he feels that he may get rid of if they get to Pune. Navin and Pooja were also happy.

Pune Again

They shift to the Pune.

For them it was like the first year after the collage and they join the company. They start the routine as they used to do it before Bangalore.

They used to work daytime and meet in the evening. On the weekend, trips, mall, movie. They were using their quality time in this period.

Sham used to smoke secretly from her. He stops to buys the packet. Once she finds out the lighter and he fake it it's his roommates and forgets in the pockets as he asked to come up with that in office. Anu didn't speak about it. She was really happy that they were together.

CHAPTER 18

Pandemic

Two and half years passed of job life. And new year start.

It was like this year was going to be best one. Everyone was really happy for it. They welcome it very cheerfully. Everyone was wishing another 'Happy new year.'

But it was the end of first month and get the news that the neighboring country is hiding something and there are such things found was the really dangerous. Lots of precaution was taken by that country.

And everything just changes in few weeks.

It turn out that was a new variants virus is spreading all over the world and it was life taking. Before this, there was a lots of virus were there like Ebola, swine flu, monkey pox, zika, bird flu. But they never turn out to be on so much extent. This was totally different. It was spread all over the world and it's was rapidly getting contagious.

First it was looking like a normal flu or diseases but as they were getting on high number of patient with death, the entire sudden all wakes up. Peoples get frighten, government was trying hard to handle the situation.

It was declared as pandemic.

COVID 19

Covid was contaminated by the droplets and air particles of viruses. Transmission was spread through the eyes, nose, mouth, and contaminated surfaces. There were symptoms like the fever, cough, fatigue and loss of taste and smell. There were not specific medicines for this disease and not the vaccine. It was spreading rapidly. The prevention method was face covering, quarantine, and hand washing. Diseases was usual on set in body was 2-14 days. And treatment was followed in that period as per the symptoms.

The entire world just stops. Everyone starts avoiding the social and physical contact. Using the mask becomes the necessary, Washing hand repeatedly was the only prevention method and avoiding social activities was the important to avoid spreading.

In just few days Government forced the lockdown in all over the country. Everything just stops. Offices, companies, school, temples, everything stops. Sudden lockdown makes the confusions among the peoples. Some were thinking it would be get away in few days and some were start to head towards the homes.

All the companies tell their workers to work from home as possible. Sham and Navin family also tells them to come home. But they both think it will not turn out on large extent, it will be disappear in few days maybe in month. So they stay in Pune and start to work from home. Anu and Pooja also start to work from home.

Everywhere was confusion out there. The new virus patients were starts to found at every state and they were implementing lockdown. Trains, bus, airlines, auto, taxis stopped in sudden.

On social media, there was new words start to flow like quarantine, isolations, pandemic, remdesivir, lockdown, hydroxychloroquine. Everyone start to wearing mask. Some were wearing even in the house. Police start rounds in every corner of the city to avoid the social gatherings. Peoples who were roaming outside were fine or punishments. This was everywhere in world. And for all, was the new challenge to live safe.

Shams cigarette packet was about to end. He made arrangement with the seller and said him to keep the more packets. He meets him, pays and takes from it.

They were both working from room. Other roommates were gone to their hometowns. There was Sham, Navin and one who didn't get the bus ticket, stay at the room. Flat owner didn't want to lose the money as he gives permission to live as long as they want. But also warn them to take care of inside and outside precautions. They used to cook the food. There was a time period for the medicals and some shops open for public.

That was really hard time going through it. Lot of bad news was getting from the affected areas. On large scale the patient were found. On social media there was good, bad, true, false every type of post were circulating. There was lot of peoples start to experiments start to make themselves safe. Some of them were trying to make the hacks to go through this situation. Some of them were showing their skill in this period on social media.

This was like war conditions. Just everyone was fighting over staying inside the home. Staying antisocial was the only way and mask, Sanitizer, gloves was the only weapons out there.

Sham and Anu were connected through the calls. Anu was sad. Sham asked about it. She said her papa has been appointed for the duty in this pandemic. It was like they were on the battlefield.

Sham calls to his home. His dad gets the weekend leaves due to spreading of the virus in their town. They said, It became the containment zone. And it was becoming the high risk zone there. And not come there. Those who are coming from cities were suspecting as the virus spreader.

Sham and Navin were about to go home but now it became the more risk so they stay on room. And also there was so much restrictions and formalities out there they drop the plan for it.

Days were passing and the situation became more critical. On the large highest scale peoples were affected and also there was deaths numbers. Big hospitals were forms. The isolations wards made. COVID ICU started. Trains also started their coaches as the hospitals. Prime minister, Home Ministers were trying hard to tackle with this pandemic. They were making their best for this situation. They give the instructions to the hospitals and doctors to give their best. Also were giving advisory to public to stay at the home and stay safe.

And the last packet of cigarette finished. Sham became cranky. His used to be mood swings. He became so irate at some point he shout on the Navin for nothing. Navin gets that what's happening and warns him not to be angry on him without reasons, It's his problem, And he can't do about it. Sham again fights with him. When he became calm. He gets that and said sorry to him. Navin avoid him.

After a time, Sham was making fun of himself and Navin told him to quit the cigarette. It will be good for the himself. Sham laughed. Navin said at least 'try.' Control mood. Try to be calm in situation.

Sham start keep his mind calm. He found it was difficult. He calls to Anu. Sham was talking with so much lovable talking Anu thinks something wrongs and she calls to Navin. Navin tells her the situation and Anu feels good that at least he is trying. They used to talk for long. after work time they were spending time to call, Chat, video calls. For Anu Important thing was, to stop the habit.

Changing the own mood was not the only reason for Sham. But also for Anu because she was upset for his dad were outside and working in that risky contaminated zone. Sham was assuring him to be the best.

Her Dairy

16 May

Today, get up and start the TV. News. There are lots of peoples again found. Situation is becoming horrific now. Don't know when did will end. Peoples are dying. Hope this will end as early as possible. I am scared for all of this.

Work from home. They are thinking like we save the two hours of travelling so will say work more. You are at home so work harder. Great.

Sham calls. Now he is talking like new relationship. It's good. Last four months he was not so much on calls. Navin says he is not getting cigarettes. Hopefully best thing happens. I was talking with him and mummy scold. I was not eating.

Papa, still on duty. Everyone at home and they are outside. But it's really important. There are some idiots thinking this is joke. There are peoples dying and they are out as a fun..

Sham was also scared. He wanted to go home.

17 May

All day just work work work. And then mummy Eat eat eat.And then Sham hi hi hi. It's like roller-coaster. From here to there. But it's really good to work from home. That two hours of travelling and all day being in that dress. Feeling comfortable.

Papa gets home so late. Really they are working hard in this situation out there. Last day they found someone was out for cigarette. Hopefully it was not him. And don't be.

19 May

Last day papa seems to be tired. On morning they were looking little bit exhausted. And also feeling low.

They call to their doctor. and then quarantine themselves in one room. Doctors came and checked them. And also us. We all are positive now. We don't have any symptoms. But we are. Papa have little bit fever and feeling weak. They give us some tablets.

Now papa gets 2 weeks of leaves. But all day rest. And we can't go outside. So all day just sit and work as much as possible.

I tell this to Sham and he gets so much frightened. He is calling again and again. I told him that I don't have any symptoms and not much feeling weak but still after hour he calls. All day total calls 11 times.

Few minutes ago I told him I said I am okay. Still ask to video call. We talk on it. After that, he relived. But still was thinking I am lying. Showed him tablets. He asks about papa. They are okay. Resting. Last one month they were tiredly working.

20 May

Today get up. And, Sham's 'good morning' text. After six months he texted in morning. I replied it with heart. And then he calls. He was asking how I am, Having fever, cough, weakness, Taste, smell, like he is doctor. I told him I am okay.

But I am not. Having little fever. Told company about it they approve leaves. Good. At least, gets sudden rest.

21 May

Again, 'good morning' with heart. I told him having fever. Made the mistakes. Now he is calling after every half hour. Asking everything. News channels are really scaring everyone. He watches in news and then asked me like this, or like this, . He said to drink hot water.

At afternoon he was asking like did you eat, What you eat, tablets, feeling weak or not? So much questions. He is not making so much call to home than me. but still he calls me.

Now Ramayana and shaktimaan. Great. That what feels like in 90's. But still when this will be end. Feeling little tired. Sleeping.

28 May

It been four day I had not write anything. Was Feeling so much weak like never before. But now at least I can walk and do some work. Last four days were so much bad... Headache, fever, not smelling, not taste. Only those people know how it weird to eat tasteless food. And this tablets.

Except mummy and bhai. They were not feeling anything. They were working and studying as regular... Maybe they are stronger than us.

And then Sham. When he gets the time he was calling again and again. I told him I am resting so he was waiting for call. Today he was talking so nicely. Was remembering collage days. He was still reminds small things between us.

29 May

It ninth day and feeling great. Today we all are feeling great. We have normal temperature, not feeling tired, Smell and taste not yet but it will clear in coming days, doctors said. Last night also sleeps well.

I Told Sham about it and he relived. About a half hour we talked on video call. He seems happy. Cracking lames jokes. But still he looks at me, I remind the first time in collage when he get scold at that same type was looking at me. He said 'when this will end, we will meet.' I Hope so.

Papa also feeling better.

2 June

Today doctors say our tests are negatives. So much relives. Papa, also feeling like good. And they said now they can go on duty again. Mammy feels angry. She said to take more 2 days leaves. Papa didn't listen to her. They are joining tomorrow on duty.

I was so much bored about this tablets and mask and staying home all day.

Sham calls. I said him I am corona negative. He was happy.

10 June

In morning Sham calls. He said there are 3 patients found in his building. He was scared. After some time he calls again asking he feels like chest pain something. I called Navin he said he had acidity. Drink ENO now he is all right. After some time Sham calls and say everything is fine. But didn't tell about the ENO.

On news, It is really spreading. And some peoples are celebrating. They are taking lightly.

All day work. So much stressed.

11 June

Sham calls in morning. More peoples were having symptoms, And whole building was under test. And they found more. Sham and Navin too positive. They have been sent to Covid center. First they were both scared but there they became relaxed. I was worried about him.

But then he calls and tells that he is fine there. He has mild symptoms. Also he gets leaves so it like holiday there. They are getting food there so all time they are just rest.

I tell them will feel little weak but in 4-5 days it will be clear.

12 June

Sham calls. He has high fever and body pain. He was barely even talking. We just talk for 5 minutes. He was weak. Navin told me he is little bit scared for this. He is telling to take rest. He is not eating food as it tasteless.

13 June

Today we didn't speak as he was sleeping all day.

14 June

We talk for 5 min and he is feeling body pain and fever. He was so calm like never before. He asked to meet me.

18 June

Today he was feeling good. Fever is down. Body pain is still. Smell and taste gone, so eating forcefully. We talked for half an hour and he told all days summery in that. I feel good that he is fine now.

24 June

Today they are at Room. They are negative now. We talk for two hours straight and he was so much talking talking and talking. He also was laughing on small things. I ask him to video call. And he gets so much happy.

After COVID

Sham and Navin came to room. They were feeling weak after that. Sham was feeling low. Cigarettes made him weak. They start to work from home. In break he used to talk with Anu.

Once, Anu's papa went to visit them at their flat. On call Sham told Anu that he feel very great for their gesture. Actually Anu said them to visit.

In city, there was still corona increasing at higher rate. Lots of peoples were getting affected. There was large number of peoples also getting well. But still there was a small amount of death number was. It was horrific atmosphere there.

Sham used to call Anu in free time. Sometimes, video calls. They both used to talk freely. Sham was eagerly waiting to meet her, but situation out there was not possible. He gets upset for this.

Also he was thinking to go home. But at hometown there were still patients but in low numbers. There was strict lockdown, also peoples who were going inside there, they have to stay outside at school for at least 15 days, If there are no any symptom then they will be at their home. School was specially arranged to stay who came from outside. There was no direct entry in the home.

Sham was getting really impatient to meet Anu. He used to call her at any time and Anu will be working at same time she would hang up. It make him upset. Anu tells him to spent time on social media to time pass.

There were lots of talented peoples were making lots of content. He starts to spent time in that. But it makes him loose concentration in work.

November

The patient rate was lowering down. The fall in new cases were showing the better situation. Also the lockdown was also unlocked for large extent. Shops will be open for day but at night there was curfew. Wearing mask was still compulsory. Social distancing was also said to be follow. Shops hotel were also given permission to be open with the large gathering. It was like normal out there.

Sham asked Anu to meet. She also wanted to meet him. But due to work and household chores, she was busy. Still one day they arrange to meet.

Anu came at the coffee shop. Sham was already there. They both sit in front of each other. Order the burgers and cold coffee. He was not talking much more but looking at her with tenderness. Anu was talking in continuous flow. Sham was listening to her.

Her nose ring was shining due to reflection of light. Sham was looking at their.

"Are you listening or not?" Anu asked as she gets that Sham was not paying attention.

"Yeah, Right?" Sham said.

"What?" Anu asked him again. Sham chuckles. He gets that Anu caught him.

"I asked you about the marriage." Anu said.

"Ok" Sham again chuckles, smiles and said. Anu looked at him pointlessly. Sham gets that something is wrong here.

"Sorry I really was not listening." He said sorry for this.

"What wrong. Is there something on my face?" Anu asked as she thinks there was something wrong Sham was looking at.

"No. No. It's like, just..." Sham was about to say something but stop himself.

"I was talking, aunt who looked groom for me, He is in Hyderabad, Multinational company. And she is asking repeatedly." Sham feels nervous as she said. Now he was looking at her with serious face. Then he starts to look down.

"I reject it." Anu laughs.

Sham also smiles. But there were not feelings in it. He was forcing himself to be look fine.

"I will not leave you. I am not idiot." Anu continues. "What?"

"Nothing, something in my eyes." Sham said as he was rubbing his fingers around the eyes. Hiding tears.

"Stop. It will get more. Take me look at it." Anu moves forward. And start to look at in his eyes. Everyone in café was looking at them. Sham take looked at them, he fells awkward.

"There is nothing in there, just let me blow in eye."

"Anu, everyone is looking at us." He said and grabbed his hand. Anu takes a look at café. She embarrassed and sit down in his seat. Sham gives her smile. Anu hides his face with the palm.

Sham was feeling relaxed after a long time. Now he was talking and Anu was listening to him. After six months they were meeting personally. Both were gone through the COVID treatment. It was hard time between them and now when the meet, they don't wanted to lose it. For the 2 hour he just forgot all his tension, pain, another world.

They both eat and came out of the café.

"Let's go" Anu said.

"Where?" Sham asked.

"Just get on bike." Anu said. Sham sits behind her. She starts the bike and they came near the temple which was near to the place. Anu parked bike. And they came inside the temple area.

Both enter in temple. Sham looked at her. She was standing, closed hands. Eyes were closed. She was mumbling something. Sham looked forward. Close his eyes. And open it. After some time Anu open his eyes. They both came out of the temple and sit on the bench which was around.

Day was about to end. There was saffron color in the sky. Mild incense sticks smell was making atmosphere fresh. Temple bell was adding beautiful tone. People were going in the temple. Also some of them sitting in the area of temple and talking.

Sham looked to his left. And old man was sitting there and looking at both. He feels weird. Sham smiles at him. He didn't change his face. Sham finds it wrong.

"Let's go outside."

"Why. It has been 5 min. You want to go room early?" Anu asked while looking at watch.

"No, just like..." He stopped talking.

"Sit, Look it really feeling fresh here." Anu grabbed his hand and forcing to sit beside her.

"No, Uncle sitting at left looking at us." Anu moved his neck to left. As Anu looked at him he changed his face direction.

"Sit, don't look at him. And if there will be problem, I will call papa." Anu shows him mobile and said. They both start to laugh.

They both sit there for long time. Without talking. They both were feeling peace just sitting there. After some time, it was late so they both came out of the temple. Drink again tea. And then Anu drops him at his room and went to home.

Sham was walking towards the room. He was thinking a lot something. His head was full of thoughts. Come near the tea stall around his room. There was guy who was smoking. Sham went to shop and gets the cigarette and tea. He starts to smoking. Maybe six months later he touches it.

Cigarette was about to end and his mobile rang.

'I reached at home. TC' Sham read the message.

'OK.' He replied.

Now he was thinking that he shouldn't have smoked that cigarette. He feels bad. He threw the cigarette and drink tea. Pay the bill and came to the room.

Navin was working on his laptop. Sham gives him the package of burger which he brought along. Sham gets fresh. Navin was eating. Sham sits in front of him. He told him everything whatever the Anu said. And at last he told him about the cigarette.

Navin asked him. He told him as feeling like stress so smoke it. Navin was angry because at after along trying he was avoiding it. But he understands the situation and stays silent. He just said to keep control on that and stay away from it. Sham agreed.

After some days Sham and Navin both planned to went home. It had been so long time. And also situation was under the control. But still there was some restrictions were.

CHAPTER 19

Home

In that week, they came home. They still were doing work from home. It was not the problem for the work schedule.

At home they had made the arrangement to stay in school for 14 days. They would get the food by tiffin there. They didn't show any symptoms so after the 15 days they enter in the home. Those 14 days Sham and Navin feels like a year.

Everyone at home was happy for them. They both used to do their work at day shift and in evening on the beach. Lockdown was fully unlocked but still gathering was prohibited. There would be no rush on there. The day when he went on the beach after so long time, He feels like alive. Last two years were so much exhausting only he knows.

Waves were moving front and back. Big red spot was about to dive on that line. Navin was beside him. He feels something. Close his eyes. The waves sound was reminding him the Ajanta.

"We should go again to Ajanta." Sham opens his eyes looked at the Navin and said.

"What happened?" Navin asked.

"Nothing, just like..." Sham mumbled and quiet.

Someone calls him. He was at home. He looked back. She was there in saree. May be he remind that blue color.

'Anu' Sham said.

And he gets up. He picks his mobile which was beside him. It was 5.30 in morning. All were sleeping. It was cold in air.

He opened his mobile. Sent ♥ in message to her.

"Sleep, you have to work tomorrow all day." It was papa whose sleep disturbed by the mobile screen light.

"Yes." Sham said and sleeps.

In morning Sham gets up. Anu's message was there. 'Call me.' Sham gets tooth brush, paste and came at backside of the home. He calls her.

"Hi..."

"You remind me?"

"No, I was sleeping."

"Not now, at night. What happened?" She asked. Sham get that last night he sent the message her.

"Sham?" She asks again.

"No I mean it's not how you think."

"Then what were you thinking at late night."

"I will complete that file today and sent you ok..?' Sham said. Sham's mummy was in front of him. She was listening them.

"Friend." Sham answered. Mummy nodded and went inside house. Sham gets that mummy caught him talking.

"What happened? Which file?" Anu was asking as she didn't get what happen there.

"Nothing. Mummy was there that's why."

"Give her phone I want to talk." Anu said.

"Shut up, just tell me, why you text me to call?"

"You remind me at night, you tell me." Anu shouts on call.

"Ohh,, Ummm , I saw you in dream , that why.." Sham tells the truth.

"Wow, now I am coming in your dreams, soooo late."

They start to fight on call in lightly comedy. About 10 minutes they were talking. Sham was in garden. After the call, he washed his mouth and came inside home.

Mummy was making breakfast. He sits beside her. She gives look at Sham.

"What?" Sham asked.

"That girl last time you came up with." Mummy guess.

"Haan..." Sham blush and said.

"Marry her." She made it in two words. Sham was looking at her with shock. She starts to laugh. And then he also starts to laugh.

"What happened.?" Papa who came in kitchen looked at them and asked.

"Nothing, just get your breakfast and go to work." She said and made their plates.

Sham would work all day and evening spent time with the friends. He was feeling good there. City rush was not there and the dusky air also. The everyday regular prefect life was ruined by the COVID.

At night again Sham sleeps breaks. Sea was roaring. He turned on mobile. It was 5. He sent another ♥ to her and sleeps.

In morning, He gets up. There was message.

'If you are missing so much badly, let's marry.'

'*K*' Sham sends.

'*When?*' He gets another message in short. He sends ☺ to her.

The both stay there for month. After that Navin came to pune and Sham stay at home.

About an month after Navin calls Sham and ask him where is he. Navin's mummy told him that Sham is not at home, He went month ago to Pune. Navin don't get that.

He calls him.

Sham was staying with his friend at around 100 km far from his hometown. It was industrial area and his friend was working there. He used to live with other workers, but they were not so much friendly. So he asked Sham to stay some day with him. He used to work in day shift at that time Sham was also working from room. After that they used to go on walk to nearby places. And then came home. Eat and then time pass. But he didn't tell Navin about it. Navin was shocked because Sham never ever keeps any secret something like this.

On call Sham tell him he forgot to tell him. And he just give company as he was their friend. Navin said him to come Pune as possible. Anu was also shocked. Till that day he was telling her that he is at home.

CHAPTER 20

Pune again

On weekend Sham came to Pune. Navin asked him what happened. He tells 'everything fine.' After that day Anu calls him to meet.

They meet in the café. This time she sit beside him instead front. Sham was quiet.

"What happened?" Anu holds his hand and asked.

"What?" Sham asked surprisingly.

"You behave like different guy than I used to meet before." Anu explained while looking at down. Sham didn't say anything.

"I am feeling scared." Anu starts to sob.

"Why?" Sham asked.

"You said you missing me then I said to come here. And for a month, you stay at somewhere and tell me that you are at home. Why.?" Anu gives the reason why he was upset on him. She was about to cry.

"He was just friends of us. Nothing else. He say came to there as for sake of old days."

"Why you told lie that you are at home, and Navin didn't know about this?" Anu asked furiously.

"See, Navin went pune. After three four days later he called me, and I didn't told because you will think wrong something. Don't think too much about it." Sham gives his answer on this.

"I am not thinking too much about this, you are..." Anu leaves his hand.

"Can we eat? I am hungry." Sham said silently.

Anu gets up and start to walk. Sham was looking at her. She was angry. And he was helpless.

He also came out of the café without eating.

He starts the bike. In between at the temple he stops. Park the bike and sit on that same bench. After a long time he turned on the mobile open the message box. Type '*SORRY*'. Think for some time and then delete it. Turned off the mobile, and leaves from there.

Came at tea shop. Get cigarette and tea.

He came on room. Remove cloths. Enter in bathroom. Turn on shower. Cold water was passing through the body. Made him calm. Changed cloths and went to the bed. Didn't even eat. Cold water made him to sleep peacefully.

At night Sham sleeps break. He gets up. He Feels like hungry. He searched in tiffin. There were three pieces of sweets. Eat them and sleep. Check mobile again. His eyes filled with the tears. He hides his face in pillow. Pillow was getting wet.

Anu came to home. Get fresh. Changes her cloths and directly went to bed. It was not like they fight before but this time Sham changed the whole topic in sudden. That made him upset. He was trying to avoid something. Maybe the marriage thing was bothering him. She was trying to sleep.

Mummy calls him to eat. She said she was not hungry.

At night she wakes up. Was feeling really hungry. Check fridge. There was leftover food in there. She eats that cold food. Get on the bed. She checked the mobile. There still was not the message or call anything. Turned off the mobile and tried to sleep. Her eyes filled with the tears. She hides her face in the pillow. Pillow was getting wet.

After that for the month they both didn't talk with each other. One day Anu get call from Navin that Sham was badly ill and now he is okay and recovered. He is on the room now. Sleeping. Anu talks with the Navin and in evening she made plan to meet them. Sham was unaware about this.

When she came near the room, Navin told to Sham that Anu is there and wants to meet you. Sham look through the window, Anu was there across the road waiting for him. Sham told Navin to come along with him.

They both came outside. Anu shares smile as she looks at the Sham. Sham smiles with the embracement. They sit in the café. The café was fully occupied and last corner seats were free. They sit there. Anu sits beside him. She order the coffee. Sham asked for the cold coffee. As the way he was walking, sitting, talking Anu gets that he is in pain. But throughout he was hiding it.

"What happened?" Anu asked him and place her hand on his hand. He moved his hand.

"Look if you don't want to talk, I should go then" Anu said softly.

Sham looked at her. His eyes were deep and look like he was not sleep properly. There were dark circles around eyes. His face was low as he was in pain. He was not talking as regular. He was like energy less.

"First drink this; it seems like you feeling weak." Anu moved the coffee glass towards him and said.

"No, I am fine just the acid reflux and the body pain. Nothing else. Now I am fine.."

Anu looked at Navin. Navin still didn't touch the coffee and it was getting cold but he also was not in mood to drink it.

"Navin, what going on here...?" Anu looked at him and asked.

"Ask him, I am just here to company." Navin said and start to drink his coffee.

All three were just stay quiet for short time.

"I really don't know but, he is hiding lots of things" Navin keep his coffee mug on table. Look at the Sham. He was looking at him.

"What's wrong with you, you are not talking with me. You stay there for a month with that Prakash to just having cigarettes. The day you came here, smoke it like a packet. He goes down at least 10 times. Drinking tea like water. Not eating food properly. Not sleeping properly. All night just stay awake watching something. And if ask then 'Its ok'"

Navin told whole scenario in one time. Sham was looking down as he doesn't get how to tackle that.

"Now five days ago, He falls weak. Whole night and day, stomach and body pain. Don't want to go to the doctor. When he can't bear it then we went there. He checked and gives the medicine and then he is recovered. Doctor said to stop cigarette and tea. Its making him like burning inside...."

Anu looked at him. Sham was avoiding his eyes to her. He was ashamed.

"And he had drink." Sham was shocked after listing him. Anu also looked at him with wide eyes.

"What, Prakash told me everything." Navin said with serious voice.

"No did not have drink. He is lying. Let me call him." And he gets up. Now he was looking like a fine man.

Anu hold his hand and tell him to sit.

"Look. He is lying, we know you had party there but you don't drink. He just is fooling you." Sham looked at Navin. He was laughing.

"Navin, Ok now. Sham...Look, why are you so nervous about everything. I am with you; Navin is with you, mummy papa. Everything is fine. **I know last two years we are not getting increments.** But it's still fine. We have good paying jobs. Whatever is in my hands; I am doing it with full heart. Just don't bear it alone. Speak it if you have any." Anu was talking with broken accent. They all stay quiet for some time. Coffees were getting cold.

"Say something." Anu asked.

"Look there is nothing about to worry of. I was there to just have little quiet for some time, you know like break. Nothing else. It was his birthday so we had a party but I swear I didn't drink." Sham explained what going on there.

"You are feeling stressed?" Navin asked.

"No, I just want to be alone for some time." Sham said.

Anu stay quiet. She didn't get what to speak. She gets upset. Sham puts his hand on her hand. They both were looking at each other. There was lot of in their eyes wanted to tell each other. But still were not able to speak.

"I will not do this again." Sham said.

Anu nodded. Her corner of the eyes filled with the tears. Sham feels bad. Anu nudges her head into his shoulder and closed her eyes. Sham get that she is been hurt by his words. Navin was also sitting with the sad face. First time he was having conversation like this with them. To change the scenario Anu break the silence.

"I am really feeling hungry."

Sham smiles. He orders the grilled sandwiches. They were eating but it was not so tasty. Not the fault of sandwiches, the emptiness was.

They talk after that for some time. And then was about to leave. Anu looked over cafe. Luckily there was no one in the café. Anu looked at the Sham and calls him. Sham leaned at her. Anu gets towards him and she kissed on his lips. And then moves backwards.

Sham was looking at her. She was blushing.

"I love you" Sham said while holding his hand.

"I love you too" Anu said and hugs him.

"I am not going to pay for this drama." Navin said as they were having their romance.

Sham laugh and paid the bill online.

Anu went to his home.

Sham and Navin also came to the room. Sham went to the bed for the rest. He lay of his body on bed slowly.

"You still have the pain?" Navin asked as he thinks still having back pain.

"No I am fine." He said.

"Why are hiding all this. Suffering all alone. We are good friends from childhood. We studied together, played, fun all together and now you are keeping all alone inside your head." Navin sit on the bed and was talking looking in his eyes.

Sham gets up. Pick up the water bottle, Drink a lot. And then sit on the bed. He was looking at the Navin he was sitting across him and waiting for the answer.

"I don't know, but feeling scared." Sham said.

"Why?"

"I really don't know. She is also with me but still..." Sham stop.

"But..?"

"Will she will be happy, or her family?"

"She likes you, her family also. Didn't tell you this but lots of times we met before. Today she just came on one call because she cares for you. She kissed you because she loves you. She feels you." Navin said as he was giving him support.

"It's not like that. Okay, we are all good at this, but someday if someone asks her that there was a lot of guy out there who are better than me. **In their community.**

Then..?"

"I don't get it." Navin asked as he didn't get what was Sham wanted to tell him.

"Means, She said there is someone out Hyderabad guy is better than me and he is from their community... There will be something always be in their mind that they could have better than me"

"Why you are compare that guy with you..."

"Because they will look at me as the outcast.....""

"She is looking for you..." Navin compete the conversation.

Sham stays quiet. He was not having any words after that.

"Look Sham, everyone is going to be comparing all time with another. She chooses you is an important. She want to be with you is really matter. Don't stress about all this nonsense. Just stop being idiot, don't do these crap things, and just focus on work. Everything will be all right."

"And if you want to talk, Just talk as we used to talk before. Don't just make mess in your head."

Sham get that Navin can understand the situation but can't relate with it.

"I am feeling low." Sham said.

"Sleep for some time. You will be fine."

I was not aware her name, surname, religion, cast when first time I saw her. I don't even care about when we were together for last 6 years. But now when we are planning to move forward this relationship, all of the sudden I am thinking what the others think about us.

Are we living on our terms or on another's one interest?

I know we can live together a great life but in their eyes she marries to another one would be more perfect.

But who would the really happy?

April.

Everything was great. Patients of corona were low. Lockdown was fully unlocked now.

And then second waves hit. Again that lockdown, Quarantine, hand wash things comes. Vaccination was also following by the government. The good thing was it was second time so everyone knew how to deal with it.

Sham and Navin were working from home. Anu and Pooja were also working from home. Sham used to call her before the sleep. All day he would work and spent time on social media. Anu used to wait for the calls. Sometimes she would call him and talk for some time.

In two months situation became normal. This wave was also dangerous but don't last for long time.

Around July, Situation became so normal again.

Sham and Navin used to be like stranger in the room. They would only talk when something necessary. Beside the work, Sham will be sleeps all time. Navin would be in confusion that he is really sleeping or just acting to be in sleep. There was always headphone in the ears.

Anu calls him, and he didn't pick up the call. Navin would tell her that he is sleeping. Once Anu asked him to meet but Sham avoids it saying he has some work or something. Anu said 'Ok".

It was rainy season. Sham was watching rain though the window. Kids were playing in the park. He was seeing them. He reminds his childhood days. He gets out of the room. Come to the tea shop. Gets the cigarette and tea.

One day, he just randomly asked to Navin to visit somewhere. Navin suggested to the Singhgadh ford. He agreed immediately. They plan for the Sunday and on Sunday they went there. Fort was closed on that day because of heavy rain but it was so much refreshing ride. Hot tea with chilled cloths.

CHAPTER 21

The End

21 July 7PM

Anu's mobile rings. She was working in kitchen. Mobile was on charging. Maybe it will not be that important call, she ignored. Again mobile rang. Anu stops chopping vegetable and get the mobile. It was Navin on call. She picks the call. She was about to speak 'Hello'. Navin sacredly voice came out.

"Anu Just come to the city hospital. Sham had an accident. Badly injured, just came."

Anu got shocked . For the second she can't feel her legs. She moves backward and there was chair beside her, she sits on it. She feels like she can't breathe. Anu's papa was there. The looked at her and Ask... "What happened?"

Anu was still in shocked. Her mobile was in his hand about to land on ground. There was little voice coming out of it. Anu's papa gets something wrong there. They get near her. Get the mobile. The call was ended.

Anu was sitting on chair trying to say something. Words were not getting out of her mouth. She was trying hard to say something to her papa. They put her hand on her shoulder and ask again. They get that there surely something bad happened.

"Sham..." words just came out of her mouth.

"What happened to Sham?" papa asked as they were supporting her. She was shivering. Tears just came out of eyes and she start to cry. Anu's papa called her mummy.

Anu's mummy come and stand next to her. She didn't get what was happening there. Anu burst into tears.

"Sham, Accident...." Anu said again.

Her papa gets the situation. They tell her mummy to bring the water. And they were moving their hand on her face and telling her not to cry.

Anu's mummy came with the cup of water immediately. Anu hands were shivering. Her mom helps to drink it.

Anu looked at her papa and said. "Papa, Sham is in the hospital, Accident...." She again stops saying something.

Her both parents get the shocked for the short. But her papa handles that carefully and asks her.

"Where are they now?"

"City hospital."

"Hurry..." They just said and from drawer, get the keys of the car. Anu's brother was studying in next room came out and he was unaware of the situation ask them, what is happening there.

"Look, we are going to hospital. Take care of home, we are coming." Her mummy said to him. Anu's papa was about to tell her to stray at home, But they think she will be needed the console the Anu. They sit the car. Start it. Car was heading towards the Hospital.

Anu and her mummy were sitting backside of the car. Anu was not crying but she was looking terrible. She was just composure that there will be nothing happened and everything is fine. Her mummy was moving her hand around her face.

Car stops at the signal. Anu's papa looked in backside mirror. Anu was sitting so much silent, it killed them. Very few times they had seen her daughter so much sitting with that quietly. Anu slides her head in her mummy shoulder. And start to sob. Her mummy was grieving her. She feels bad for her.

Signal turns green. Car start.

They came at the hospital. Park the car and came in front of the hospital entrance. With shivering hand Anu called Navin.

"Where are you?"

"Ask someone where is ICU." Navin told.

As she listen ICU. She was about to fall. Her mummy gets her. They get her near the bench and her papa hold mobile and start to talk.

"Where are you?"

"Outside ICU" Navin get that it her papa.

Anu's papa said to stay both there. Get her water. They will get the situation. Anu was about to stand up. They force her to sit.

"I will get him, Just stay here. OK?" Her papa said and they moved towards the man who was wearing like hospital outfit. "Where is ICU?"

"On the left, There." He said. Anu's papa runs towards it.

There was Navin and another guy outside the ICU. There was two another police men out there talking with each other. Anu's papa gets towards the Navin.

"Anu?" Navin asked as he didn't see her.

"She is devastated. Sitting at the entrance. What the situation here?" Seeing policemen they just get little bit in tension.

"He will..." He moved his head in no. and moves down his head. He was all broke.

Anu's dad put his hand around his shoulder.

In between Anu and her mummy came from behind. Anu was still crying. Anu's papa panicked for some time. The moved forward. Hold her hand and were trying to sit on bench.

"What happened papa, Why Navin is crying?"

"Sham had an accident. Little bit of injured. But okay now. You stay calm. It will be okay."

"Why ICU?" She looked at them and asked.

"Beta, It's an accident. Maybe there will be internal injuries, they are checking him. Be brave. Okay?" Anu's papa looked at the Anu's mom and with the eyes they tell her to handle Anu.

Anu's papa came near the Navin. He was still standing looking at the Anu. "His family informed?"

"Yes, they are coming. Will be here in morning." Navin said.

"Okay."

Anu's papa moved towards the Policemen.

"What's the situation?" They asked to one of them.

"Are you relative of him?" One of them asked.

"I am GOVT servant in RTO. The guy inside, I know him."

They showed their card. They both get that he is an upper officer. They tell them to come beside.

"Sir, Drink and drive case. Bike was on full speed." Other one said.

"But he didn't drink."

"He was. And bike slipped. It's major. I don't think will be alive." He added.

"You sure?"

"Not sure, but there lot of blood out of him at spot. And lot of injuries out on body." Another one said.

Now Anu's papa gets the whole situation on his eyes. He feels like horrifies. He didn't get that how to tell about all this to the Anu. They looked at her. She was looking somewhere in zero.

They came at Navin. Navin was tensed. Anu's dad sits beside him. That environment was really terrific.

"How do you get this?" Anu's papa asked.

"We lived near. Someone came and tell me that your friend had accident and they moved here and then I came here and got him." Navin said.

"He talked to you anything before it..?"

"NO, actually he used to smoke..." Navin stop. "Means, he used to go outside sometimes alone on my bike. As usual I think he went." Navin completes.

"He was drunk?" Anu's dad asked him awkwardly.

"No, He never drinks. He never did anything like that. He hates it. Cigarette ok. But still he didn't light up in front of me, never. But Drinking. No Never..." Navin said confidently.

Anu's papa looks at Anu. She was sitting with her mummy. Her head lay back on her mummy's shoulder. He stops crying but little sobbing. She was sitting quietly. It was look like she was thinking so much about something.

"What was with him?"

"I don't know sir, Last three four months whatever he was thinking, doing weird. He used to go out somewhere, Sometimes even in night. Used to come late. But never saw him drinking. Used to work properly but after that sleeps or go outside. But today I just..."

Anu's papa gets up. He pats his shoulder to support him. They sit beside the Anu. Anu moved his head on their shoulder. She was all broke inside.

After some time doctors came out of the ICU.

They came near him. They think maybe they are patient's relatives. Anu closed his eyes as wanted to change this entire situation.

"It's critical, but we will try our best." They said silently.

"Ok doctor." Anu's papa said.

Anu didn't listen to it.

She was thinking too much about anything else. They didn't even eat food. It was 9 PM in night.

11.30 PM

Everyone was sitting there so quietly that the machines beeps were only sound making it scarier. Anu was awake. She didn't talk with anyone in last two hours. All she was looking at the ICU and looked somewhere. On both side her mummy and papa was there. They both were exhausted.

After sometime. Navin gets near her. He stands in front of her.

"Anu..." She didn't listen to him.

Navin looked at the Anu's papa. "Sir, you three please go home. We are staying here. You are tired and hungry too. Get rest for some time."

Anu's papa looked at her daughter. They called her, but only lips move, there was no sound. They pat on her shoulder. Anu feels like someone touch her. She looks. There were tears in her eyes still.

"Beta, we should go home. You work all day and you tired too. I think you should rest."

She was speaking something but she troubles. She picks up the bottle of water beside her. Takes sip and said.

"You go home and rest. I will be here."

Anu's papa looked at the Navin as will confront her. Navin gets that.

"Look Anu. We will be here. You go home now. Rest and came on morning. You are tired; it looks on your face.

And also will be hungry. Go Home. We are here. Don't worry about him, he will be okay." Navin was telling because she was really looking like powerless.

Anu was not in state to go home.

"Look beta, Everything will be all right. Now we should go home. Look papa really need some rest." Mummy said. Anu looked at them. Papa would not leave her there alone. If she stays, they also will be stay with her. So she agreed. They start to return home.

They came home. Anu's brother made the khichadi. Anu didn't eat it. She directly went to the bed. All she was shatter completely. She closed her eyes. ICU red board just came in front of her eyes. The hospitals walls, the beeps, Running peoples all were coming in front of her eyes.

She gets up. She was feeling very low. Get the bottle of water. Drink a lot. And then check the mobile. He saw Sham chat box. There was his message 'I LOVE YOU' few days ago. She was about to cry. She hides his face in pillow and start to cry.

7 AM

Anu didn't sleep at night. She was awake all night. At around 5 AM something, because of tiredness she falls asleep. She gets up when her papa enters in the room. Anu's papa were didn't sleep well. All they were care about the How Anu going deal with it.

She gets up. Call the Navin. Navin tells her Sham is still in ICU. His mummy and papa are there.

After some time, Anu and her papa went to the hospital.

Sham's mummy, papa were there. His mummy was crying bad and his papa were supporting her.

Navin and his friend were so much tired. Whole night they just stay awake. There was no chance to get the sleep at that atmosphere. All night just machines sound and hospital rush. Their eyes were become blue.

Anu sit beside on next bench where Sham mother was. Anu looked at her. She was all sobbing. Anu's papa were talking with Sham's papa. And then they went to their office.

After some time Doctors' visits again and then they came out of the ICU. They walk towards the Sham's mummy and papa. Talk with them. After that his mummy fainted. And papa hold her and helps sit on the bench. It was like they all lose the hopes for him. They both breaks.

Four hours after, Nurse calls doctors again. Doctors rush and something happens inside. After the hour they came out of the theatre. They calls Navin and place his hand on his shoulder and nod their head with heaviness on face. Navin's eyes filled with tears.

Anu was looking at them. She gets what's happened. She was about to cry but one hand just slipped around eyes and try avoids the tears.

Navin came near the Sham's papa and mummy. He sits in front of them on knee and looks in Sham's papa eyes. And nod his head into no.

After some time doctors came again. They were talking with the Sham's papa about something. Anu came forward. Doctors said his eyes are still fine because of helmet; they can donate it to someone. Someone can see the world...

Anu said to Sham's papa to donate it as they he can see after his life.

They agreed.

CHAPTER 22

Affliction

After some days,

Navin Gives, diary to the Anu. It was the same diary Anu gave him as a birthday present few years ago. She opens it. On every page there was something written.

Shayari, quotes, gazal, memories ...

Navin said he is packing Sham's things. Maybe this belongs to her.

Anu closed the diary and put it in the purse.

"I got call from hospital. They give eyes to some child and he can see now. But they didn't get any other information."

Anu looked up. Navin and Pooja were looking at her with tears.

Anu smiles.

They make them more painful seeing her like this.

"Anu, take care..." Navin said.

Anu smile again, nod her head and start to walk.

Navin and Pooja were behind her...............

Continue...